Elizabeth Mayhew Waller Edmonds

Greek lays, idylls, legends

A selection from recent and contemporary poets

Elizabeth Mayhew Waller Edmonds

Greek lays, idylls, legends
A selection from recent and contemporary poets

ISBN/EAN: 9783337152246

Printed in Europe, USA, Canada, Australia, Japan

Cover: Foto ©Andreas Hilbeck / pixelio.de

More available books at **www.hansebooks.com**

GREEK LAYS, IDYLLS, LEGENDS, &c.

A SELECTION FROM RECENT AND CONTEMPORARY POETS.

Translated

BY

E. M. EDMONDS.

WITH INTRODUCTION AND NOTES.

Revised and Enlarged Edition.

LONDON:
TRÜBNER & CO., LUDGATE HILL.
1886.

TO

MISS FLORENCE M^cPHERSON,

IN WARM APPRECIATION,

AND WITH THE ESTEEM WHICH KINDRED SYMPATHIES

INSPIRE,

This Little Volume

IS INSCRIBED.

PREFACE.

In making a selection from the works of recent and contemporary Greek poets, the desire has been not so much to represent the individual poet as the people whose voice he is. The array of names held in high and deserved estimation by their countrymen, and the amount of literary production, whether in drama, epic, or lyric, is so great, that any attempt to give a just representation of the modern Greek poets through the medium of one small volume of translations is impossible. It is possible, however, by collecting a few national and descriptive poems, to illustrate the feelings and characteristics of the people by whose almost unguided efforts the War of Liberation was carried on.

As the springs and founts of this unexampled rising had their sources deep down in the affections and religion of the people, so by the side of historical and other episodes relating to the struggle for freedom I have placed legendary poems, folk-songs, and other lyrics containing any cherished customs, which, whether derived from archaic or Christian epochs, have been from time to time so gracefully clothed in verse by several living poets.

Such having been the intention, however imperfectly carried out, it is naturally to be expected that a greater number of pages would be devoted to Aristotle Valaôritês than to any other poet; for Valaôritês is without dispute the most truly national poet of Greece, who, whether he is narrating one of his country's tragedies, or describing an individual grief,—chanting as it were an Epirote myriology,—he is through and through, alike in language as in thought, *the poet of the people.* Although a gentleman by birth and a man of the highest cultivation, he identifies himself in his poems with the peasant and his wild fancies—the patriotic Klepht of the hills,—the free-hearted brave sailor of the ocean, and the devoted bishop or monk pouring out his blood for his country and its faith. His poems may in many of their phases be objected to as presenting too often a realistic picture of human suffering, unnecessarily prolonged painful details, and almost, as it were, a revelling in horrors; yet even here he is a true delineator. Through ages of oppression a quick, sensitive people, ever alive to receive impressions, had been made familiar with scenes of brutality which had produced the effects not only of a partial obscuration of former perceptions of the bright and beautiful, but also in the emphasizing in words as in thought an intense hatred of the oppressor. The tendency to unnecessarily lengthened description of suffering is not confined to Valaôritês,[1] but is also conspicuous in other writers. The old Greek προσωποποΐα, a remarkable feature in Epirote folk-lore, is seen almost as a religion in Valaôritês. Birds, trees, rocks, and waves are all in sympathy with the patriot and hero. The above remarks apply in a less degree to Julius Typaldos, who ranks only second to Valaôritês as a national poet.

The metres and forms of the originals have been adhered to in every instance where the spirit of the originals does not suffer by too literal a treatment. For the long unrhymed hexameter I have mostly substituted rhymed endings. In the gruesome poem of "Thanasy Vayia" I have employed changes of metre more capable, I thought, of pourtraying in our language the weird pictures there presented.

Throughout I have avoided the admixture of Greek words. "Manna" and "Manoula," although eupho-

---

[1] For this reason I have omitted some lines in "Thanasy Vayia," which are indicated; also the concluding lines in "The Bell."

niously pretty, are not preferable in their English dress to "Mother." The same may be said of many charming diminutives, which, if more homely in the English equivalent, are at least more intelligible to readers not familiar with modern Greek. In the spelling of proper names I have also, out of consideration for the same readers, written them as nearly as possible as they are popularly pronounced. The present volume has been enlarged by "Supplemental Poems," consisting of short specimens from Chrystopoulos, Solomos, and Vlachos, with the "Elegy to George Gennadius," by Zalakostas, to which is added a Biographical Note by his son, Mr. J. Gennadius, and Additional Notes and Appendix.

Notwithstanding the much to be regretted position which Greece has lately occupied, the consequences of which may possibly retard for some time the steady progression depicted in Mr. Jenkyn's Introduction, I allow this to remain as it first appeared, firmly believing myself that the future of Greece will yet be worthy of her liberty-loving, industrious, and intelligent children.

ELIZABETH MAYHEW EDMONDS.

July 1886.

CONTENTS.

[1] In "The Flight" and "Kleisova" I follow the versions in Matarangha's "Parnassos," which omit two stanzas in the first part of the former poem, as also the love episode in "Kleisova."

PAGE

Poems of Sentiment and Feeling.

Legendary Poems.

[1] All the poems by Mr. Viziénos are taken from "Αἱ Ἀτθίδες Αὖραι" (Trübner & Co., 1884).

Love Lyrics.

Folk Songs.

From the Εἰδύλλια of GEORGE DROSINÊS.

———+———

ATHANASIUS CHRYSTOPOULOS, the son of a priest, has earned
for himself the title of the "Modern Anacreon." He was
born in Macedonia in 1770, and was at an early age taken
by his father to Bucharest to study, and from thence went
to Venice and Holland. Returning to Bucharest, he held
many honourable posts there as an instructor ; and, in
1836, desiring to pass the rest of his life in Greece, went
to Athens, but not being able to bear the heat, returned
again to Bucharest, where he died in 1847 (pp. 268, 269).

DIONYSIUS SOLOMOS, who has achieved his celebrity chiefly
through his "Hymn to Liberty," was born in Zante in
1798 (living to see the fruition of his patriotic poem), and
died in Corfu in 1857. His minor poems are character-
ised by simplicity and grace. His education was for the
most part carried on in Italy (pp. 265, 266).

GEORGE ZALAKOSTAS, born in Epirus, went with his father,
when nine years old, to Florence for his studies. The
eventful year of 1821 (he being then eighteen) called him,
together with his father and brother, to Missolonghi, to

take part in the struggle. His patriotic poems are often
narratives of his own personal experience. He never left
the army. His death in Athens in 1857 was accelerated
by his grief at the untimely loss of seven out of his nine
children (pp. 51, 151, 265, 275).

ALEXANDER SOUTSOS, born in Constantinople in 1803 ; died
in Athens in 1863. He studied at Chios and Paris, and
his first compositions were in the French language. He
cannot in justice lay claim to the title of "Father of
Modern Greek Poetry," which has been accorded to him
by some. The neglect which his countrymen bestowed
upon him and his brother Panagiôtes during their lives,
and the penury which accompanied them both throughout, may have called forth this overstatement in tardy
acknowledgment of their merits. The poetry of both
brothers shows the undue influence of the French school
(p. 65).

JOHN KARASUTSOS, born in Smyrna in 1824, and dying in
1873, seems by the accounts of contemporaries to have
endured throughout life many sorrows. His poems have
been described as breathing all the sweetnesses of Ionia,
but they are somewhat wanting in force and originality
(pp. 155. 181).

ELIAS TANTALIDÊS was born in Constantinople in 1818 of
needy parents. His intelligence and insurmountable per-
severance overcame all drawbacks. He studied both in
Smyrna and Athens with the greatest success, and devoted
all his powers to philology and philosophy. Nothing
daunted by his blindness, which occurred in 1845, when
he was only twenty-seven, he still continued working, and

in the year that succeeded this calamity was chosen Professor of Greek Rhetoric and Literature at the Theological School at Chalkis, a post he filled for thirty years. He died at Constantinople in 1876 (pp. 130, 161).

ARISTOTLE VALAÔRITÊS, the most national poet of Modern Greece, was a native of Leucadia, and died in 1879. He belonged to an old Epirote family. His studies were carried on at Corfu, Paris, and at many universities of Western Europe. He afterwards fixed himself in the Ionian Isles, where he interested himself in politics. To him and to Achilles Paraschos only among modern Greek poets does the eminent critic Roïdês accord the gift of the highest genius (pp. 32, 82, 89).

JULIUS TYPALDOS was born at Lixuri in Cephalonia, and was educated in Italy, graduating at Padua. Upon his return to his native land he was admitted to the bar, eventually became judge, and for some time held the post of President of the Correctional Tribunal in the island of Zante. Later on he was nominated a member of the Supreme Council of Justice, which office he held up to the end of the English Protectorate. After the union of the islands with Greece, Typaldos retired to Florence, where he wrote much. He died, however, in Corfu in 1881, whither he had gone only a few months previously, full of years and in failing health. His only collected poems was a small volume published in Corfu in 1856, and long out of print.[1] Many of his poems are found in collections without their authorship being apparently

---

[1] A public library at Corfu, and also a Greek gentleman from his private library in Athens, generously and synonymously sent me this volume as a loan.

known, as for example iu the " Anthology of Michael-opolos," Atheus, 1885, there will be found " The Two Flowers," called there " Maria," as if from the pen of an anonymous writer (pp. 25, 118).

CONTEMPORARY POETS.

[1] Now generally written Vizyenos; but I retain the form which the poet used in his first letter to me, which was in the English language.

INTRODUCTION.

Many interesting books have been written upon modern Greece, but very much of the most valuable information is contained either in expensive works, or in volumes now out of print, and therefore inaccessible to the general reader. This being the case, comparatively little is known in this country of the history of the War of Independence, in which our fathers took so lively an interest.

As this little work may fall into the hands of some —more especially the youth of both sexes—who have not had their sympathies awakened by the many deeds of daring of the Hellenes during that eventful period, it has been deemed advisable to add to the value of the notes appended to some of the poems contained herein, by presenting a few sketches calculated to show that the modern Greeks are not the degenerate race some Turkophiles have represented them to be.

Space will not allow any long series of narrations,

whether of individual or collective heroism, in which the War of Independence was so rich; a cursory glance only will be given at three tragic episodes—sufficient in themselves to exemplify the spirit of the whole history of that time—viz., the fates of Suli, Chios, and Missolonghi.

In the poem in this collection called " The Flight," we are taken back to a period immediately preceding the general rising of the Greek peoples—a period when the brave Suliots maintained their sturdy independence against all the forces led for their overthrow by Ali Pasha of Epiros. Notwithstanding Ali's defeat as recorded in the poem, he, as soon as his arrangements were complete, renewed the struggle with his wonted energy.

His troops, composed of diverse elements, mustered at the least 20,000, chiefly Mahometan Albanians, who were stimulated to fight in their master's cause by a clever revival of an old Mahometan prophecy, that an Albanian empire would be established upon the ruins of the Turkish power, which latter, from various causes, even then showed evident signs of rapid decay and collapse.

In the heroic defence of hearth and home, the brave people of Suli could not muster, at most, more than some 1500; but the sacredness of their cause animated them with almost more than human courage. Even women and boys fought against the common foe.

Where all made themselves conspicuous in repelling the fierce onslaughts of Ali's troops, it would appear invidious to particularise persons. History, however, has left on record two names, towering above their fellows as "the bravest of the brave"—Photo Tzavellas, a son of the Lambro of "The Flight," and the good priest Samuel, who was known indifferently as the Caloyero or Papás by the mountaineers.

During the period under notice this remarkable man arrived at Suli: from whence nobody seemed to know. His antecedents were a mystery, and remained so; but he came to throw in his lot unreservedly with the hardy mountaineers. By his fervent Christianity, coupled with the extraordinary devotion he exhibited to their cause, the Papás in a very short time gained the entire confidence of the people, and was appointed their polemarch or minister of war. He fulfilled all the duties that devolved upon him as a Christian priest, whilst at the post of danger he was ever foremost; no wonder then that the Suliots came to look upon him with awe, and this feeling would not be diminished when we bear in mind the remarkable title of "η $\tau\epsilon\lambda\epsilon\upsilon\tau\alpha\acute{\iota}\alpha$ $\kappa\rho\acute{\iota}\sigma\iota\varsigma$"—"the last judgment"— by which he designated himself in his proclamations and addresses to the Suliots.

The Greeks, ever allured by the marvellous, crowded round him with enthusiasm, and followed his footsteps from village to village, whilst he proclaimed amongst them "the fulfilment of time," "the overthrow of Kedar," and the approaching "glory of the remnant of the Lord."

His ascetic piety, his wild and prophet-like aspect, his fastings, his preachings, and above all, the purity of his patriotism, served to endear him to his companions. During the last close investment of their mountain strongholds by Ali's forces, the Suliots had to undergo the greatest privations, being at one time reduced to such straits as to be compelled to subsist for a while upon grass boiled with a little meal. The end however drew near, as Ali found means by corruption, to accomplish what he had failed to do by dint of arms; but even in their direst extremity the Suliots were able to obtain terms, viz., permission to retire to Parga, and compensation to be given for the large quantity of gunpowder still in their magazine. The transfer of this latter was undertaken by the brave Caloyero, who remained behind with five companions for the purpose, whilst the inhabitants left in companies, under the different chiefs.

The last act of the Caloyero was in full keeping with what had gone before, and proved that the confidence reposed in him had not been misplaced.

When the negotiations were concluded, he was asked by Ali's secretary what treatment he expected now that he was in the Vizier's power (who, it should be added, purposed having him flayed alive): the reply was characteristic of the man. "He can inflict none," said Samuel, "that can have any terrors for one who has long hated life, and who thus despises death," suiting the action to the words by discharging his pistol into a barrel of gunpowder upon which he was seated. The terrific explosion which followed shattered everthing into atoms, one Greek alone escaping.

It would take too long to follow the poor Suliots in their retreat. Harassed and cut off by Ali's forces, comparatively few ultimately reached a place of safety; but Photo Tzavellas shone with additional lustre on account of the skill and bravery he exhibited in conducting the band under his command through so many dangers. It has been deemed right to treat thus largely upon the Suliots, as their protracted defence and heroic conduct in the last extremity exercised a great moral influence on the minds of the Greeks everywhere, and very materially prepared the way for the War of Independence by teaching the down-trodden Christians their strength.

In the deadly contest that soon followed, when the whole Greek nation rose in arms to recover their freedom, innumerable examples of heroism present themselves to our view.

The Greeks rose against a tyranny of 400 years' standing, the greatest evil of which was that it tended to make its victims well nigh as debased and as barbarous as its ministers. In thus considering the position of the Greeks, it is much to their honour that they had virtues left—that they had sufficient valour, sufficient unity and constancy to carry on the struggle at all.

During the reigns of the Sultans immediately following the fall of Constantinople, one cannot doubt but that the oppression of the Greeks was far less than it was under their miserable successors in later periods. The early Sultans were mostly great men and great rulers; their government was vigorous, and if stern—often cruel—it was far from being always unjust. With those later detestable tyrants and voluptuaries, in whose characters weakness and wickedness were combined, the Hellenes became exposed to the exactions and insults of innumerable subordinate despots, and could no longer, with the same confidence, "flee from petty tyrants to the throne." One privilege after another was curtailed, or withdrawn altogether, until at last it was made penal to teach a Greek child either the language or the religion of his fathers.

In order to keep alive the fire of Hellenism and save the nation from being altogether lost in a flood of ignorance—moral, intellectual, and religious —it would seem as if God put it into the hearts of the leaders to hold night assemblies for the purpose of instruction; and we are forcibly reminded of this in the little song "φεγγαράκι μου λαμπρός."

> "O pretty little moon,
>   Shine out and guide my way;
>   And while I steal to school,
>   Let not my footsteps stray.
>   There knowledge good to us is given,
>   A precious gift sent down from heaven."

Concurrently with the revival of learning, commerce also, from various causes, began to attain large dimensions in the hands of Greeks, many of whom, by their successes as merchants and traders, amassed large fortunes.

This reacted upon the country in such a way that educational institutions increased with so much rapidity that every Greek community possessed a school where their youth received instruction not only in the vernacular, but often also in the ancient language. Very shortly the public press came to make itself heard in the number of works issued therefrom on history, poetry, philosophy and science, which were eagerly read by all classes of the people. With this influx of commerce, and the spread of education, the long-lost voice of patriotism began to be heard, and the desire to free their country took possession of the Klepht on the mountain side, the mariner on the ocean, and the peasant in the field; and it is perhaps to this *aroused intelligence* of the nation (combined with the advance of commerce) more than to any other cause that we must trace the origin of the Greek Revolution. At this period we find the advent of such men as Koraes, Rhigas, and others.

The former, whilst encouraging his countrymen in resistance to the Turks, did not fail to plead their cause before Western Europe, and endeavour to enlist sympathy in their behalf. Of his literary labours it has been said that no country except Germany could show his equal. He laboured to purify the language and reduce it to fixed rules; and it was ever his aim to elevate the moral qualities of his countrymen.

Rhigas, known by his spirited heart - stirring war-songs, fairly electrified the whole population of Greece, and they rose as one man to fight " for the holy faith in Christ and the freedom of their country."

A prominent (and unique) feature in the War of Independence is the utter absence of any real leader on the Greek side; the movement was essentially one of *the people*, and throughout their fiery ordeal we fail to come across one real chief claiming either the confidence or the obedience of the nation. With the exception of Ypsilanti and Mavrokordato, and perhaps two or three others, the leading characters were men from the crowd. This has left its mark down to the present time upon the Hellenic kingdom, where titles of nobility are still not to be found. Even such an adverse critic as M. About has paid the Greeks an admirable compliment on this score.

From the toiling class we have a glorious roll of names. Amongst others, the most perfect characters are Andreas Miaoulis, the great naval commander, who is said to have been " an iron man, who never smiled and never wept," and who after his victories retired and lived as a private citizen; Markos Botzares, the simple-hearted descendant of an ancient Suliote family; and Konstantinos Kanares, who claims a special interest in that he serves as a connecting link between the far-off past and our own times, living long enough to hold office as premier of his country under King George, and surviving until A.D. 1877, full of years and honours. How the then youthful sailor avenged the butcheries and rapine committed by the savage Asiatic hordes on the peaceful and defenceless inhabitants of Chios (a home of learning and civilisation), will be repeated in the language of Gordon:—" The fast of Ramadan ended on Wednesday the 19th, . . . and the Grand Admiral [of the Turks] celebrated on the night of the 18th, by a splendid entertainment, the approach of the moon of Bayram, which he was not fated to behold. Surrounded by the blood-stained trophies of Scio, he had forgotten the vicinity of the Greeks, who, since their previous failure, lay in the harbour of Psarra, meditating a plan for his discomfiture. We have now to narrate one of the most extraordinary [naval] exploits recorded in history, and to introduce to the reader's notice, in the person of a young Psarriote sailor, the most brilliant pattern of heroism that Greece in any age has had to boast of — a heroism, too, springing from the purest motives, unalloyed by ambition or avarice. The Greeks were convinced that if they did not by a decisive blow paralyse the Turkish fleet before its junction with that of Egypt, their islands must be exposed to imminent danger; it was proposed, therefore, in their naval counsel, to choose a dark night for sending in two *brulots* by the northern passage, while at each extremity of the strait two ships of war should cruise in order to pick up the *brulottiers.* Constantine Canaris of Psarra (already distinguished by his conduct at Erisso) and George Pepinis of Hydra, with thirty-two bold companions, volunteered their services; and having partaken of the Holy Sacrament, sailed on the 18th in two brigs fitted up as fire-ships, and followed at some distance by an escort of two corvettes, a brig, and a schooner. They beat to windward in the direction of Tchesmè under French and Austrian colours, and about sunset drew so nigh to the hostile men-of-war, that they were hailed and ordered to keep off; they tacked accordingly, but at midnight bore up with a fresh breeze, and ran in amongst the fleet. The Psarriote *brulot*, commanded by Canaris, grappled the prow of the Admiral's ship, anchored at the head of the line a league from the shore, and instantly set her on fire; the Greeks then stepped into a large launch they had in tow, and passed under her poop, shouting, "Victory to the Cross!" the ancient cry of the imperial armies of Byzantium. The Hydriotes fastened their brig to another line-of-battle ship carrying the treasure and the Reala Bey's flag, and communicated the flames to her, but not so effectually, having applied the match a moment too soon; they were then picked up by their comrades, and the thirty-four *brulotticrs* sailed out of the channel through the midst of the enemy without a single wound; they had, however, in their bark a barrel of gunpowder, determined to blow themselves up rather than be taken. While they departed, full of joy and exultation, the roads of Scio presented an appalling sight. The Capitan Pasha's ship, which in a few minutes became one sheet of fire, contained 2286 persons, including most of the captains of the fleet, and unfortunately also a great number of Christian slaves; not above 180 survived. . . . Although the Reala Bey's ship got clear of the Hydriote *brulot*, and the flames were extinguished on board of her, yet she was so seriously damaged as to be unfit for ulterior service; and the *brulot,* driving about the roadstead in a state of combustion, set fire to a third two-decker, which was likewise preserved through the exertions of its crew. Overwhelmed with despair, the Capitan Pasha was placed in a launch by his attendants, but just as he seated himself there, a mast falling, sunk the boat, and severely bruised him; nevertheless, expert swimmers supported Kara Ali to the beach, only to draw his last breath on that spot where the Sciote hostages had suffered!

" For three quarters of an hour the conflagration blazed, casting its light far and wide over the sea and coast of Asia, and alarming even the city of Smyrna. . . . At 2 o'clock on the morning of the 19th, the flagship blew up with a dreadful explosion. It would be difficult to paint the consternation of the Turks : all vessels cut their cables, some running out of the southern channel, others beating up towards the northern. . . . From such desolation, we turn with pleasure to a subject worthy of delight and admiration ; the triumphant return of Canaris and his valiant companions. It was a proud day for Greece when those intrepid men, entering the Psarrian harbour amidst the firing of cannon, ringing of bells, waving of banners, and the acclamations of the seamen and citizens, doffed their slippers, and walked in silence to a neighbouring church, to render thanks to Providence, which had granted to thirty-four champions so signal a victory over the infidel host." (Gordon, I. 366.)

This was not the only act of daring performed by Kanares, and his intrepid courage evoked universal admiration. His epitaph was pointedly written by Wilhelm Müller, and thus translated into English by Professor Aytoun, many years ago :—

> " I am Constantine Kanaris,
>   I who lie beneath this stone ;
>   Twice into the air in thunder
>   Have the Turkish galleys blown.
>   In my bed I died—a Christian,
>   Hoping straight with Christ to be ;
>   Yet one earthly wish is buried
>   Deep within the grave with me :
>   That upon the open ocean,
>   When the third Armada came,
>   They and I had died together,
>   Whirled aloft on wings of flame ! "

This and other bright examples did not fail to produce fruit in the steady growth of Phil-Hellenism, and we find such men as Byron, Murray, Gordon, Hastings, Church, and Cochrane, with a number of other distinguished persons from various countries of Europe, taking their place among the native defenders of Hellas. But what undoubtedly contributed more than anything else to gain the sympathy of Europe and accelerate practical intervention was the fall of Missolonghi—a name which will ever be associated with that of Lord Byron. And what heart capable of any generous emotion does not kindle at the name of Missolonghi? Month after month the little band of heroes in the city beheld land and sea covered with the camps and fleets of the Turks and Egyptians. Yet not a man dreamed of surrender; what men with arms in their hands could dream of it, while they saw priests, and women, and children writhing on the stake beneath the walls? At last came that terrible night, that fearful sally which will live in the pages of history as long as the world stands. During the last three weeks of the siege the chief articles of food had been sea-weeds and the leather of their shoes, which, softened by a little oil, was almost regarded as a *delicacy*. In the streets there were seen lying old and young, men and women, sick, famished, or dead. To save the remnant, it was resolved to make a sortie, and on the night of the 22d April A.D. 1826, out of 3000 men the bravest warriors were selected to force a passage, sword in hand, through the whole hostile army surrounding the devoted city. A number of others unable to follow either from age or disease, or unwilling to leave their beloved homes and the tombs of their ancestors, assembled near the powder magazine, and calmly awaited the end.

When the moment arrived, the Greeks best able to fight took the lead, being followed by all the young men at arms. *All the women* were likewise armed, and *disguised as men*, many carrying a sword in the right hand, and an infant either in the left, or fastened to their backs. They were followed by the old men, women, and children, under the protection of a body of soldiers forming the rear. When at last the order was given in a thundering voice, " Forward ! forward ! death to the barbarians !" with superhuman courage the vanguard of the Greeks rushed on the fortifications of the enemy, and nothing was able to stop their progress. Not the savage hordes of Reshid, not the disciplined battalions of Ibrahim the Egyptian, could endure that desperate charge. However, some one shouted out " Back into the town !" and great numbers were driven back by terror. With these the Arabs and Turks entered the city, and fearful scenes were enacted, which lasted the whole night. The Greeks fired the magazine, and next morning Missolonghi was a blackened heap of ruins, among which some 3000 Greeks were buried, together with many thousands of their enemies. Of those who cut their way through, only some 1800 succeeded in escaping to a place of safety, the remainder having fallen heroically as martyrs in the cause of liberty.

Missolonghi fell, but her ruins served to draw the attention of all Europe to the fact that it was high time, in the cause of humanity and justice, for the Western Powers to put an end to a conflict that had raged so long and so relentlessly. At last Greece became free. Since its independence the little kingdom has passed through various vicissitudes. It has been left to our own times to witness an enlargement of its borders; when the next extension of its frontier will take place it is beyond our province to forecast. That she is capable, however, of bearing an enlargement, and thereby to take a more forward place in the council of nations, no true observer can gainsay.

The kingdom is making steady progress commercially and educationally; life and property are safe; and under the wise administration of King George the state of Greece indicates a steady following in the path of the more advanced countries of Western Europe.

From the very nature of the Greek insurrection, when a whole nation rose in revolt against their oppressors, those comprised in the rising embraced, as might be expected, very different elements: they were, however, of one mind in defence of their faith and fatherland. The Klephts formed no inconsiderable part of the fighting element, and upon many an occasion did valiant service. They knew intimately every defile and mountain - pass. How well they utilised this knowledge history records in the total destruction of not a few well-disciplined and brave Turkish battalions.

One might expect that these Klephts, exposed as they were to constant dangers, living mostly in inaccessible places, often spending whole nights with no covering over their heads but the heavens—who in regard to elements of self-denial closely approached monastic austerity—should, from the very roughness of the life they led, be entirely wanting in acts of kindness, and given to deeds of vindictive cruelty.

To judge them so, however, would render them great injustice. If they were implacable in their enmity towards their oppressors, no acts of revolting cruelty have ever been charged against them: the ball, or dagger, speedily and surely put the foe out of pain. To their friends they were faithful to the death, and many are the stories recording acts of the utmost devotion and humanity on their part. It should be also mentioned to their credit that notwithstanding the many inducements offered to the contrary, they clung tenaciously to the religion of their fathers, apostacy among them being a thing almost unknown.

It would be both unjust and ungenerous to omit in this crude sketch, *special* mention of another class who took a noble part in the war, viz., the *Greek women*. The females of Suli handled the musket with dexterity, and when danger ran high, stood side by side with their fathers, husbands, brothers, and sons in many a hard-fought engagement, Moscho, the wife of Lambro Tzavellas, being particularly celebrated for her bravery. It would be a long category to record the many names that suggest themselves, some of whom, like Despo's, have been enshrined in song. Bobolina, a wealthy and heroic Spezziote, not only fitted out a number of her own vessels against the Turks, but commanded in person and participated actively throughout the war, invariably showing great courage. Of a different type, but none the less serviceable to the cause, was the refined and accomplished Madalena Mavroyenis, the heroine of Mykonos, who spent a fortune in alleviating the wants of her distressed compatriots, and whose many sacrifices and devotion will make her memory ever dear, not only to every Hellene, but also to every one who appreciates pure and disinterested patriotism.

But undoubtedly the most striking instance of all, was the part taken by the women in the defence of Missolonghi, to which allusion has already been made, and to which our special attention is called in the poem, " Our Grandmother's Girlhood." That this historical poem is not a creation of fancy, or the description of an isolated case, will be self-evident when it is borne in mind the number of women who must have been in the city at the time. Of the valiant 1800 who survived the horrors of the terrible night of the sortie, nearly 200 were women, who like the brave old lady forming the subject of the poem, had literally *to cut their way* to freedom!

Justice also demands that these remarks should not be brought to a close without stating how much the Greek nation owes to the Orthodox Church.

The very existence of the Greek nation is, more than to any cause, due to the existence of the Orthodox Church. The profession of the Orthodox faith was the distinguishing badge of the Byzantine Empire for the last six centuries of its existence. It was to those who held it instead of a nationality. So, too, in later days, under French, Venetian, and Ottoman bondage, religion and nationality have ever been identified in the Grecian mind. When the Greek, either from interest or other causes, ceased to be an Orthodox Christian, he became denationalized, and invariably sided with the oppressors.

A member of the Latin communion, or a Moslem of the purest Hellenic blood, ceases to identify himself with the Greek people: the Cretan Moslems, the most oppressive of all, were of Grecian origin; the Latins of Syros, throughout the War of Independence, openly sympathised with the infidels against the Orthodox insurgents; it was by the hands of Christian Mirdites that Botzares met his glorious end. Consequently to the Hellene, Greek and Orthodox are synonymous terms. The bishops and priests, when the time for active resistance came, were the first to lead the Greeks against the tyrants. And who suffered more cruel tortures than the clergy? They were amongst the first martyrs in the struggle for liberty and religion.

Gregory [1] the Patriarch of Constantinople and the Bishops of Ephesus, of Derkos, of Nicomedia, Thessalonica, Adrianople, Anchialos, and many other hierarchs, were hanged in different quarters of the capital, and their bodies, after having been exposed during some days to the insults of the Turkish rabble, were cut down and surrendered to a mob of Jews, by whom they were dragged through the streets, and afterwards flung into the sea. The Archbishop Germanos was the first who raised the standard of liberty near Patros. It was the Bishop of Rygon who,

---

[1] Gregory the Patriarch was offered life, wealth, and honours, if he would declare himself a convert to the creed of Mahomet. He repelled the suggestion with scorn, and bade his executioners cease from insulting the servant of the Crucified. After that he spoke no more save in aspirations to God. His lifeless body, floating on the waters of the Bosphorus, was picked up by a Russian vessel, and conveyed to Odessa, where it was buried with great pomp. On the fiftieth anniversary of his death the Greek nation succeeded in having his body brought back again into their midst, when it received its second burial in the Cathedral of Athens, the funeral oration of the martyred Patriarch being delivered on the occasion by the learned and eloquent Archbishop of Syros and Tinos—Alexander Lycurgus, since gone to his rest. [See Miss Skene's "Life of Archbishop Lycurgus."]

during the prolonged sufferings of the siege of Misso-
longbi, encouraged the besieged by his heroic example
to fight like lions. Numerous other ecclesiastics took
part in the struggle whose characters may well be
summarised in that of the Bishop of Helos, of whom
it has been said that "with every external sign of
humility, he was a *real* enthusiast, *always ready to
preach or to fight,* and consequently had an extraordinary influence over the soldiers."

We find the very same spirit animating the Greek
clergy in our own times. Witness the devotion exhibited during the struggle in Crete, when the celebrated monastery of Arkadi was blown up rather than
surrender to the Turks, and the Cretan ecclesiastics,
who were able so to do, carried the rifle and bore their
full share throughout the campaign. A gentleman
who took part in the fighting in that island in 1866
and 1867 writes of one popular priest—a representa-
tive of his class—that "the spirit of a Crusader
landing on the shores of Palestine seemed to burn
within him." Yet with all this practical action in
the temporal interest of her members, the Eastern
Church has not forgotten her spiritual mission. She
has had to cope with innumerable difficulties, has
witnessed trials and persecutions, often of the most
cruel description ; nevertheless she has ever held fast
" the charge committed to her," and to-day as of old
she neglects not to pray " for the peace of the whole

world, stability of the holy Churches of God, and the union of all."

In compiling this prelude to the very interesting poetical versions which follow, the writer has not scrupled to avail himself largely of the labours of others.[1] If what is thus imperfectly put together serves to awaken sufficient interest in any reader not already conversant with the excellent works of Gordon, Tennent, Xenos, Gennadios, Lewis Sergeant, and Hilary Skinner, to go into those trustworthy sources for fuller information, the object of this introduction will have been gained.

MATTHIAS JENKYNS.

Cardigan, South Wales.

[1] In addition to the authors named later on, to whom the writer is under deep obligation, much use has been made of an excellent article which appeared in the *Edinburgh Review* for April 1856.

LAYS,
HISTORICAL AND DESCRIPTIVE.

The Young Klepht's Farewell.

—Julius Typaldos.

" Farewell ye lofty mountains, ye streams of limpid
    light,
Ye mornings bath'd with dewdrops, each moonbeam-
    clothèd night,
And you—dear Klephts—my comrades, who've made
    the Turks oft fly.
I have no illness wasting me, though I go forth to
    die,
But when the bullet felleth me my soul will yet
    remain—
A small dark bird becoming —a swallow black,
    who fain
Must go in early dawning to see you fight once
    more.—
And when the wan moon cometh out, when all
    the battle's o'er—
Then back unto the cypress-tree, with swift wings
    having flown,
I'll sit and mourn the few Klepht lads with whom
    the earth is strown—

All through the lonesome night-hours whilst they're
    lying there in sleep,
Listening to their mothers who with wailing dirges [1]
    weep."

"Lo! the Pasha's portal now is reached—so pause
    thee in thy song."

"Farewell, high hills, and rivers ever running bright
    along—
Oh bury me, my brothers, where the reeds grow tall
    and thin,
There to hear the choral nightingales when they lead
    April in ;
And when in San Sofia in the great church shall
    resound
The song of ' Christ is risen ' whilst the incense floats
    around,
To the City as a snow-white bird I'll haste to fly
    away,
And like a child of Paradise sing out my gladsome
    lay."—

These words had scarcely flown his lips, when dead
    he fell to earth.
But where they laid him in the ground a cypress
    had its birth ;

[1] Μυριολόγια = myriologics. See note end of vol.

And every day at dawning, amid the breath of
    May,
A lonely bird would go and 'mong that cypress'
    branches stay,
And look unto the East—to the City [1] gazing long,
And sing in mournful tones and low its sad and
    plaintive song.

[1] As the devout Jews have ever turned to Jerusalem with intense
longing and mourned their lost Sion, so with like regretful
affection the *true* Greeks have looked for four centuries towards *the
City* and San Sofia, which the old fragment, supposed to have
been written soon after the taking of Constantinople, so well em-
bodies in the lines beginning—
    Πῆραν κὰι τὴν Ἁγίαν Σοφίαν τὸ μέγα μοναστῆρι.

The Death of Hamkos.[1]

—Julius Typaldos.

What terror is this lone Tepleni [2] that fills.
The sun veiled in clouds passes over the hills—
Shouts of joy with loud blasphemies rising up near—
With oaths, and with wailings, and voices of fear!

She lies on her darken'd bed writhing with rage,
For now 'tis with death the stern strife she doth
    wage ;
But the same savage spirit still gnaweth the breast
Of the mother of Ali with unpitying unrest.

O Death ! quench the words from her lips ere they
    pass ;
Not yet hath the blood been outpourèd.   Alas !

[1] Hamkos, the mother of Ali, being in the agonies of a painful death, left as her dying legacy to her son (between whom and herself there was a great love), the destruction of Gardiki, for an insult received forty years previously.   See notes on Ali Pasha.

[2] Tepleni or Tebleni was first occupied by the Turks in 1401, and was an obscure town in Argyro-Castron, and owes its celebrity to Ali Pasha having been born there—"*le fatal avantage*," as M. Pouqueville recounts it.

Dismay and destruction she willeth to be—
It is slaughter—the sword—she bequeaths to Ali!

" Where art thou, my son, that thou leavest me
    lone [1]—
Ah, haste thee, for Death will now make me his own ;
The depths of my bosom are chilling and cold—
While others in joyous life festivals hold !

Every nerve in my body is thrilling with pain,
Whilst another face glows with the rose' purple stain ;
For me—there is only a bed in the earth—
While for others are wreaths, the dance, singing,
    and mirth.

Ah Son ! make Gardiki [2] a desert and waste,
A wide place of tombs, whither hungry wolves haste ;

---

[1] Ali made all the fiery haste which he possibly could command,
but did not arrive until his mother was dead.

[2] " J'avais visité cette ville florissante, J'avais connu ses familles
patriciennes. . . . J'avais été temoin de ses malheurs recents. . . .
Je fus frappé de terreur en y entrant. Je frissonais, en voyant les
mosquées abandonnées, les rues désertes et silencieuses, et le deuil
d'une ville entière, privée de ses habitants. Les pas de nos chevaux
étaient les seuls bruits, nos voix les seules intonations, auxquelles
l'écho endormi répondit en se reveillant du fond des tombeaux.
Partout se présentait l'image de la désolation, ouvrage du satrape
d'Epire. Le bains publics ouverts, les portes des maisons brisées,
des pans des murs écroulés, des rues incendiées, et pour êtres
vivants, quelques sinistres jacals, ou des chiens devenus presque
sauvages, qui, par leurs hurlements, paraissaient nous demander leur
maitre, et invoquer la pitié, voila ce qui restait de Gardiki."—
Voyage de la Grèce, par F. C. H. L. POUQUEVILLE, liv. iv. chap. II.

And drowned in their own blood be mother and child,
With old men and maids.   Fire and sword! spread
    ye wild!

Yea! fire and sword!   Be the head of the youth
From the girl's bereft arms stricken off without ruth,
And torn from the breast where yet trembling it hung,
Let the babe at the feet of its mother be flung!

Let them leave all the joys they have tasted below,
And know all the pangs of death—ling'ring and slow.
Ay—fire and sword!   Let one grave's scattered
    mould
The wreaths of the bridal—and the dead bride enfold!

Fire and sword!   But what chills are these creeping
    around;
Woe! woe!   The sun seemeth by cold vapours
    drowned—
From whence are these phantoms of dread which I
    see?—
Ye pale, headless corpses! what would ye with me?

Alas! to my bed they steal softly and slow,
And their wan ghastly heads upon me they would
    throw!
Their lips are announcing a doom of dismay—
Leave!—leave me! ye brothers of Ali![1]—hence!—
    away!

----

[1] Besides Ali and Chaïnitza, their father Veli had previous to
his marriage with Khamco or Hamco, two sons and a daughter by

He feareth a dagger in secret upraised.[1]
Beware! in thy camp, Charon seeks thee amazed;
They have planned—they have sworn—near—near
    they come on—
Woe! woe! It is *thy* blood they thirst for, my
    son!

One hath fall'n, he hath fall'n, the elder is slain,
The younger, though wounded, still struggles amain,
A forest of swords whirleth o'er him,—O Death!
Haste—haste and mine eyes with thy cold fingers
    sheath.

Pity, pity me, Death!—Not yet cometh it nigh—
I see a bare yataghan waving on high;
They have seized him, alas! by his snows' whitened
    hair,
And hurl him down—pitiless—sight of despair!

Stay! stay! but ferocious the murmur of death—
Woe! woe! 'tis *his* head that now falls to the
    earth.

a slave, who with their mother fell victims to the jealousy of
Khamco.—Dr. Holland, p. 104; also Duféy, c. II. p. 26. [Résume
de l'Histoire de la Régénération de la Grèce. Jusqu'au 1825, par
P. J. S. Duféy, 3 vols. 18mo. Paris 1825.]

[1] Hamco affected to believe that his brothers were plotting
against Ali's life.

Revenge! revenge! Moucktar! Veli![1] But behold—
Whose hand is that now those heads severed doth
    hold.

The earth is o'ershadow'd—the Shades howl with
    fear,—
What monster of Hell brings these shudderings
    drear—
It hath flung itself o'er me—I stifle—Ali!"

But Charon hath seized her fierce soul and doth flee.[2]

[1] A vision of coming retribution is here presented before Hamkos in the downfall and decapitation of her son in his old age, and of her two grandsons, Moucktar and Veli, who were beheaded by order of the Sultan some time previously, being then in revolt against their father. The poet brings so many events which occurred at long intervals in such rapid succession, and gives them so abruptly, that the translator has some difficulty in giving an intelligible reading.

[2] Hamkos died about 1790. This and the four following poems are arranged chronologically in reference to the events which they narrate.

The Flight.[1]

—Aristotle Valaòritês.

I.

" My horse ! my horse ! Omer Vrioni bring here—
The Souliote is on us—the Souliote is near—
My horse !   Dost not hear how the hot bullets pour,
And whistle around us and threaten us sore !

See'st not those demons who there on the height—
Like pebbles are hurling down heads in our sight ;
Behold now the gleam as their flashing swords swing,
And over the rocks headless carcasses fling !

My horse ! my horse !   See'st thou the slain on the
        ground—
Those are wolves which are growling and flocking
        around ;
The dark realm of death is before me, I see
The wide jaws of hell which are opening for me !

[1] This poem records the panic-stricken ride of Ali Pasha to
Janina by night after his memorable overthrow and the almost
complete annihilation of his forces by the Souliotes under Lambros
Tzavellas on 20th July 1792.   See note, end of vol.

C

Hither—Vrióni!¹—one moment—then free—
I am safe from their talons as onward I flee ;
My horse!—when I see that white kilt, well I know—
'Tis thou—Lambro Tzavell' my merciless foe!

See'st thou not ever that death follows nigh
In the face of his yataghan whirling on high ;
Well I know that one stroke from his hand at the
        heart—
All flutterings straight cease—and all tremors depart.

My horse! my horse quickly Vrióni bring here,
The sun it hath sunk and the dark night draws near ;
O save me ye stars! give *one* ray, faithful moon!
'Tis Ali Pasha now who doth ask thee a boon."

Before him careering his good horse behold,
As black as a raven, and glitt'ring with gold—
Who shows like a flame—or a swift flash of light,
Of pure Arab breed in which Northmen delight.

He heareth the battle—his ears at the sound
Stand erect, while the sparks from his hoofs fly around ;
With nostrils distended—red gleaming and wide,
He champs the bit—pawing the earth in his pride ;

¹ Omer Briónes was general-in-chief to Ali.   He was a Greek by
birth, and is stated to have served under thirty different flags
without knowing why.   His name is frequently written " Vrioni."

Forward he springs from his haunches—a flash
As his iron-shod hoofs cut the air as they dash—
Scarce touching the ground like a meteor of light.
Shame ever such steed should be mounted for flight!

Brave Lambro beholds him with envying eyes,
And he biteth his lip as he secretly sighs :
" Ah barb all excelling ! hadst thou been with me,
This day I had rode to Janina on thee."

Then stricken with terror Ali Pasha flings
One hand on the mane—on the shoulder upsprings ;
And quick as the lightning or bullet's swift flight,
Ali and his courser are lost in the night.

II.

They are fleeing—they flee—Retribution is here,
They are hunted and followed by pale ghastly fear ;
The deep swarthy night and the dark clouds alone
Their only companions—escorting them on.

Through the woods—leaping thousands of trenches
    on high,
The spurs shedding blood-drops as onward they fly ;
Like the sea in its onflow—the horse scatters foam,
Time fails—whisper fears through Ali's heart that
    roam.

Along while thus speeding, the waving of trees—
A falling leaf rustling—the murmuring breeze—
A bird on the wing—gazelle bounding away—
A streamlet that through the gorge taketh its way :—

All bringeth wan fear to Ali Pasha now—
Cold, cold is the sweat that is bathing his brow ;
The horse pricks his ears, not a sound, not a sigh,
But rigid his feet, for a wolf passes by.

Ali with his fingers his saddle grips tight,
Before him Tzavella is ever in sight ;
And in phantasy drear, all around, it doth seem
That bare blades are waving with murderous gleam.

Afar floats his beard, which is white as the snow,
And hurled by the wild wind, and tost to and fro
O'er neck and o'er mouth, as in elf-locks 'tis cast,
It looks like pale scorpions which hunger and fast.

And like as the waves by the south wind when tost
Beneath Night's dark shadows are hidden and lost,
Yet as they roll forward, their spray mounting high
Is a glitter of light on their crests sweeping by—

So thro' Night speeds Ali on his steed swift and
        strong,
Like the wave in the darkness which rushes along—

A wave heaving heavily, black as the shade,
Where the beard of Ali hath a white foam-streak
    made.

They are fleeing—they flee—as a whirlwind they're
    past,
But fears are assailing the good horse at last:
His knees are now trembling, they stagger beneath,
With quick throbs of agony pants he for breath.

Ali Pasha cursing, his weakness derides,
Still deeper he plungeth the spurs in his sides;
The horse writhes in anguish, and uttering a groan,
Makes yet one bound forward—then drops like a
    stone.

Like the strokes of a hammer his heart's every throe.
His ears they are drooping, on earth he lies low;
Still bravely he struggles to rise, *but 'tis death!*
And the blood from his nostrils is flowing beneath.

So there, where his steed in last agonies lay,
Ali stood transfixed, as the life ebbed away.
He gazeth upon him, and restless and pale,
Strains forward to listen, lest all sounds might fail.

For still he is fearing the balls of the foe;
He clutches the pistols from his girdle below—
c *

Whilst near him his courser, lying stretched on the
    ground,
Moans yet, and his hoofs tear the earth' sods around.

With noise so distressful in vain would he hear
If those demons are still in pursuit, or are near.
Ali Pasha foams—now a spark, then a flash,
And straight to that heart's depths the two bullets
    crash.

Convulsed—as appeareth a spectre of dread—
The horse gives one groan—one last groan—and is
    dead :
His eyes roll no longer with fiery glare,
But misty and dim on the high heavens stare.

III.

He heareth the footfalls, the shouts of a host !
Have the shots from his pistols betrayed him and
    lost !
Yet nearer, congealed is the blood in each vein,—
He plucks at the dead horse to raise him again !

His arms he reloadeth—one quivering hand
Is groping down softly to grasp his good brand.
He heareth his name, " Hither, Vizir Ali."
And as tapers consume so his courage doth flee.

Again there are voices, and each time he hears
That the tumult approacheth more near—still it
    nears ;
With eyes wide distended, with spirit affrayed,
" Help, Omer Vrióni, help ! " shouts he dismayed.

Ali Pasha thus pursued hotly and fast,
Like a dying man enters Janina at last ;[1]
But as long as he liveth, full oft 'fore his eyes
The white fustanella [2] of Lambro will rise.

---

[1] Ali Pasha, through chagrin, did not leave his house for a fortnight after his arrival in Janina, and forbade the inhabitants to look out from either door or window, in order that they might not learn the terrible disaster which had befallen him.

[2] The "fustanella," which I generally translate by "kilt," varies considerably in different districts. In some parts, as at Megara, it is of an ordinary fulness, but the majority still shows an enormous width. It is made of white cotton in small gores sloped from two or three inches to seven or eight at the base. The base of the one measured was seventeen yards ! The "fustanella" will soon be obsolete.

Katzantonês.[1]

—Aristotle Valaôritês.

Ye who ever saw him near you
  On the mountain ridges high,
Partridge,[2] falcon,[3] golden eagle,
  Swallows—all who soaring fly,
Come and raise the song of mourning,
  Raise for him the chant of woe ;
They have taken Katzantonês,—
  Mourn ye birds in wailings low.

Traitor priest it was betrayed him !
  When he takes the holy bread
Sword may it be then unto him
  That shall dye his lips blood red.

[1] A celebrated Klepht who conceived the idea of freeing his country before events were ripe for it, and being betrayed, was executed with his brother at Janina under circumstances of great barbarity. See note on " Katzantonês " at end of vol.

[2] The partridge is a favourite bird with Greek poets, even employed in love-songs as a type of beauty. See Appendix.

" Les bartavelles ou perdrix Greeques sont très nombreuses dans toutes les montagnes ;" "descendant en plaine pour faire son nid et couver à l'abri d'une grosse pierre."—Pouqueville, *Voyage dans la Grèce*, liv. xxi. chap. v.

[3] ξεφτέρι = *vulture;* can also be rendered *hawk* or *falcon*. See Appendix Notes.

'Round his neck a rope, and knotted,
  Straight become the sacred stole :
Ne'er for him be found confessor .
  Who shall dare absolve his soul,
Ne'er for him be loving fingers
  Which shall close his eyes with dole.

George Hasote, his valiant brother,
  Ever watchful ward doth keep—
Wakeful ever, whilst beside him
  Still doth Katzantonês sleep ;
For the fever flush is on him—
  Yea, the fever burneth high.
" Brother, wake ! upon my shoulders
  I will bear thee, and will fly—
Wake ! in slavery to bring us
  See our foes already nigh."

" Fly, and save thyself, my brother,
  Do not fret thy soul for me,
But—an' if thou lov'st me truly
  Ask I now this grace from thee—
Cut my head from off my shoulders,
  That no Arab[1] make it prey ;
Up to Agrapha then bear it,
  To some chosen rock away.

[1] Jousouf Arabe. He was the most bloody of all the leaders under
Ali, and had previously been in the service of his father Veli.

Give it to the rock to wear it,
    Make of it its topmost peak ;
Let it wear it for a helmet,
    Hold it ever—who may seek !
Come, O brother ! do it quickly—
    Quickly sever it, nor stay,
High that I may hence be soaring
    Thither high to flee away,
Where the dark clouds have their rising,
    Where the lightnings have full sway ;
When their smoke will bring remembrance,
    When their flash will call to mind
My poor gun, which now an orphan
    Leave I in your hands behind,
So that thou may'st love and tend it
    And in it thy brother find."

George then knew this was the fever—
    Knew this was the fever rave,
And he flung him on his shoulder,
    And he sprung from out the cave,—
Bearing forth his precious burthen,
    When he seeth straight in view,
Sixty fierce Albanian soldiers,
    Who with eager haste pursue.
Each time they to him were nearing
    Like a rampart firm he stood,

And 'fore Katzantonês' body
  Made defence with weapons good.
(Joy be ever to the mother
  Who such hero sons have borne !)
Thus these two most valiant brothers
  Were pursued until the morn—
Till the daystar came forth brightly,
  Which all stars then paled before ;
And when George, the brave Hasotês,
  In his foot was wounded sore,
When they took them both—and living
  Straight unto Janina bore.

So one dawning near the Plane-tree [1]
  Which from one small sapling grew,
Ever broadening—ever spreading—
  Nourished aye by blood anew,—
There with heavy irons laden
  Came they forth to meet their fate,—
From those two grim cruel doomsters,
  Their last hour to await.
Tools for thousand like achievements,
  Torches, hammers, anvil there !
Scorpions from the earth out coming !
  All they look on—all are 'ware.

[1] 'Ο πλάτανος was the place of execution in Janina for the "martyrs" to Greek independence. See " Μνημόσυνα " σελ. 95 (a). It was formerly the custom to plant a plane-tree, *platanus cœlebs*, on the birth of a male child. See Pouqueville's "Histoire de la Régénération."

George, as though he had been weeping—
  Weeping for his brother dear,
Gave one glance to Katzantonês,
  And then dashed away the tear.
Where the brothers oft discoursing,
  Where the one the other told—
By the cool and pleasant fountain
  All their youthful ventures bold,
All Ali Pasha's [1] great terrors,
  Gheka's [2] zeal and fiery glow—
Flashed a sword, on sudden waving,
  Fell a noble head full low.
" Christ is risen, I'm o'erwhelmèd,"
  Katzantonês loudly cried,
And a kiss—a deep, deep heart-kiss
  Wafted to him where he died.

'Mid the branches of the Plane-tree,
  All among its leaves so fair,
As it were unto her harbour
  Fled and hid his pure soul there ;
And it looked upon the brother
  Whom to martyrdom they bare.

---

[1] Ali Pasha, ordinarily brave and daring, was nevertheless subject
to great panics.   See Pouqueville's " Histoire de la Régénération,"
tom. i. liv. 3.

[2] Veli Gheka, an Albanian in the service of the Satrap, celebrated for his encounters with the Klephts.

Stretched and bound upon the anvil,
  Then the two smiths smote him sore—
Mighty strokes which flesh and sinew,
  Bone and muscle, bruised and tore ;
But he looked up into heaven,
  Singing as the blows he bore.—

" Smite, ye dogs, again, and hew me,
  Ye have Katzantonês here ;
Ali Pasha with fire and anvil
  Ne'er to him shall carry fear."

Then one hour long they hewed him,
  And their hands waxed faint and slack—
Yea, the smiths were both awearied,
  So his faithful throat they hack ;
And as on the sand outpouring
  Runneth forth his blood so red,
Still they hear his song uprising,
  And its words in dying said—

" Smite, ye dogs, again, and hew me,
  Ye have Katzantonês here ;
Ali Pasha with fire and anvil
  Ne'er to him shall carry fear."

Then the Plane-tree through its rootlets
  Straightway sucked his blood within,

Greedy, yet with understanding
  Lest the earth might drink it in.
Thus there followed thence a harvest,
  And it spread its branches wide—
Spread them strongly, yet in quiet—
  Tufted foliage o'er each side,
Which Ali Pasha beholding
  In his dreams at dead of night,
Shouted loud to bring the torches
  Lest had come that day of light,
When the branches of the Plane-tree
  Will crush the City in their might.[1]

[1] There is a vast and distinct difference between the mountain
heroes in revolt, who, with *the priesthood*, kept alive the seeds of
freedom, and those robber bands who, like the Mohammedan Albanians under Ali and his father Veli and others, became rich by
inroads on peaceful inhabitants, although historically they are equally
named as Klephts. "Dans les villes maritimes le commerce grec
prospérait, mais pour les hommes de l'interieur, nulle issue que la
montagne. La montagne, ce que dans les pays organisées on appelle
le brigandage, ce que le monde officiel dans toutes les capitales
nomme le rebellion. La montagne pour les Grecs était l'inde-
pendance, la continuation de la lutte nationale, la guerre sans merci
au conquérant dont on n'acceptait pas le joug. Ce que s'est
depensé d'heroïsme, de courage, d'opiniâtreté indomptable dans
les combats que, pendant des siècles les Klephtes livrèrent aux
musulmans, on ne le saura jamais. Les gorges des montagnes, les
rochers, et les forêts ont gardé le secret des spectacles dont ils ont
été les temoins. Les chants transmis de génération en génération,
ont seuls conservé la mémoire de quelques uns. Nul n'a le droit
de laisser périr dans le souvenir des hommes le nom des héros qui
ont combattu pour la patrie comme l'on fait les montagnards de la
Grèce."—JULIETTE LAMBER, *Les Grecs Contemporains.* Paris.

Thanasy Vayia.

—Aristotle Valaôritês.

I.

" O pity, gentle Christian hearts, have pity, God above
Will bring you consolation, and will keep you with
    His love ;
Some tender mercy show unto a widow, lone and
    poor ! "
Thus pleaded one poor woman at another's humble
    door.
" Fierce is the night and wild, I am mantled deep in
    snow ;
Must I perish on your threshold ?   Have compassion
    on my woe,
For I too worship God ! O Christians, pity ! in His
    name—
Your kindly wicket open !   Not to eat your bread I
    came—
I do not ask for bread, for I have long since learnt
    to fast.
The poor feel for the poor ! Oh save, lest Death may
    come at last !
Give but two charcoals from your hearth, or reach me
    but the light

Which you each evening kindle, which in the lamp
    each night
Burns 'fore God's holy Mother, before the Virgin high,
Pity! a little light—some light!   Ah, help me lest I
    die!¹

II.

CHILD.

" Mother, awake! dost thou not hear? at our door
    methinks some sound "—

MOTHER.

" 'Tis the wind which the boughs of the forest rends
    as it groans and whistles round."

CHILD.

" Mother, I fear, as a flutt'ring bird my heart is throb-
    bing fast."

MOTHER.

" It is but the wild dogs' howling—thyself in my
    fond arms cast."

CHILD.

" I hear loud shrieks and cries."

MOTHER.

    " 'Tis a dream thou art seeing, dear!

---

¹ For account of the infamous executant of the orders of Ali
Pasha against Gardiki, see note " Thanasy Vayia."

Turn thee around to sleep, and make thy cross, and
　　cease to fear."

III.

Mother.

" Yes, at our door some groans I hear
As of some soul in anguish near."

Straight she doth rise, and seeketh where
Low on the earth a form was there.
Pale was the face, with tresses torn
Dishevelled o'er her shoulders borne ;
And icy cold her hands were prest,
And crossed upon her drooping breast.

" Child, come hither and give thy aid,
Real were those sounds thy spirit 'frayed."

Then quickly in their arms they bear
The stranger who their bed shall share.

" 'Tis midnight, little darling ! rest
Near to thy mother's loving breast ;
And, stranger, sleep thou warm and well
Till dawning fair good omens tell."

D

To child and mother hasteth sleep,
Their eyelids closed in slumber deep ;
But the eyes of the stranger are opening wide !
What form doth stand the bed beside ?

IV.

THE PHANTOM.

" Why comest thou, Thanasy, to me here ?
Hath Hades then no sleep ?
Why comest thou to me, a thing of fear,
Before my eyes to keep?

I laid thee in the grave—I laid thee deep,
And that is now long past ;
Have pity, Athanasius ! let me sleep,
Rest—rest to find at last.

They follow me—they follow where I go—
Thy cruel, cruel deeds ;
All flee me—none will helping pity show
For thy lone widow's needs.

Stand off !   What have *I* done, Thanasy ? say,
That thou bring'st me this ill.
Pale art thou, and thou reekest of the clay !
A fleshly form hast still ? [1]

[1] ὁ βρυκόλακας is a phantom whose body having been excommunicated is not able to be dissolved in the ordinary manner in the tomb.   See notes on *Thanasîs Vayias.*

Draw near to thee thy shroud, upon thy brow
    The worm doth pasture free ;
Accursèd one ! · Behold where even now
    They fly to feed on me !

Tell me—whence art thou in this tempest drear ?
    Hark how the whirlwinds rave !
Tell me—whence art thou, that thou seek'st me here,
    And leavest thy deep grave ? "

V.

" Amid the darkness of my tomb,
    As I this night was shut in gloom,
There buried low beneath the ground,
    By the grave's narrow compass bound.

I suddenly hear the owl, which cries
    Above " Thanasy Vayia ! rise !
Thousands of corses now prepare
    To hale thee forth, and take thee *there.*"

I hear the words, my name I hear,
    My bones they chafe and snap with fear ;
I hidé me from them—crouch away
    In my deep pit as best I may.

D *

"Come out, Thanasy Vayia! lead!
    Out! to that mountain side we'll speed;
Out! out! fear not; no wolves are we—
    Show which Gardiki's road may be."

.   .   .   .

And when they found me, all the rout
    From my tomb so lonesome drag me out,
Laughing, mocking, fiercely tear,
    And as they told me thither bear.

We fly, we run, a raging blast,
    The world despoiled as on we past;
And wheresoe'er the black cloud came,
    The mountains shake, the earth's aflame.

Our serecloths swelled out in the gale,
    Like as if voyaging under sail;
And all along our path, down thrown,
    With hollow bones the earth was strown.

With trailing wing the owl before
    Screameth "Thanasy" evermore!
Until that place was brought to view
    Where this same hand so many slew.

What sight! what horrors there unfurled!
    How dire the curses on me hurled!
They gave me to drink of blood again,
    Upon my lips thou canst see the stain!

Whilst me they throng upon and haul,
They stay and listen: one doth call,
"Well met, well met, Vizir Ali!
We'll to the courtyard hence with thee."

And as the corses on him fling,
None waiting—me abandoning,
In secret hasted I and fled
Hither to share my own wife's bed."

VI.

" I have heard thee, Thanasy—no longer stay!
Tis the hour thou must back to thy tomb—away!"

" But in my grave for companions there
I must now from thy lips three kisses bear."

" When oil[1] and when earth over thee were thrown,
Thy mouth then in secret I kissed—alone."

" Long years and many since they were left,
And that kiss hath the lower depths from me reft."

" Off—thine eyes' wildness doth me affray,
Piece by piece falleth thy flesh away—
Hence, and thy skeleton fingers hide,
For they gleam like daggers displayèd wide."

---

[1] Oil is always poured over the body at Greek funerals when committing it to the grave. See note, end of volume.

"Wife, come thou hither, for am I not he—
He who aforetime was loved by thee?
Shun me not now, I'm Thanasy, thy own;"
"Hence! to the Pit thou would'st drag me down!"

 . . . .

  . . . .

He growls like a wolf—like a leaf he doth shake—
'Tis the Holy Cross which his fingers take.

Her relic hath saved the unhappy one,
In smoke from her side hath the phantom gone.

Then again without was heard screeching wide
The owl, which "Thanasy Vayia!" cried.

VII.

' Wake, darling child, awake! the dawn is coming
  o'er the hill,
Wake! let our hearth be kindled; see the stranger
  waits us still.
Good day unto thee, mother; hast thou found somewhile repose?"

" I, wretched one! sleep little, and not once mine
  eyes did close.
Farewell, farewell, good people, I must leave you and
  away,

Still onward—onward moving, far off lies my outstretched way."

" Why didst thou not awaken us, nor lone in silence
mourn ;
Good mother, give thy blessing ere thou goest forth
this morn."

" For all the loving charity which ye to me have
shown,
May the good God sweet healing sleep for ever send
you down ;
No richer gift the whole world hath—no better thing
it sees,
And day and night I seek for it, and day and night
it flees."

" Ah, mother ! sad-eyed Poverty keeps ever wakeful
lids."

" Wealth I have known, but wealth doth fail as
Time his chaplet thrids."

" We, hapless ones—like hunted wolves—we here
this refuge found
That day when lone Gardiki was low levelled with
the ground ;
Ah, woe is me—ah, woe is me—and *who* that mis'ry
brought ?

'T was Thanasês! It was Vayia! who evil foully
　　wrought."

" *Ilis wife am I.*—Good people, make your cross and
　　let me go,
Fetch holy incense—burn it—and be cleansèd from
　　your foe ;
For he this night was with us—yea, he stood beside
　　us here :
Dear Christians, weep for me, for my sad days and
　　nights of fear."

The child and mother crossed themselves, and stood
　　in dread dismay,
As from their cabin-door she turned and sped her
　　lonely way.

Kleisova.[1]

—George Zalakostas.

A Turk went down to Kleisova
  With flag of truce in hand,
And standing 'fore the walls he thus
  Out spake his lord's command :

" Sons of the Greeks, the great Satrap
  Offer of grace doth send—
To yield with honours, and withal
  Would treaty fair extend

If one there be who can discourse
  In tongue of Turk or Gaul,
Straight let him forth for colloquy
  In faith and trusting all."

[1] Kleisova, an islet in the lagunes of Missolonghi, is memorable for its heroic defence by Kitsos Tsavella with only 130 men, against the combined forces of the Satrap of Egypt, Ibrahim, and Kiutahi Rhesitês Bey. The writer of this ballad, George Zalakostas, was himself with his father and brother fighting at Missolonghi, and the poet to the end of his life devoted himself alike to the Muses and to military affairs. His poems are chiefly the narrations of the triumphs of the deliverers of his country, in addition to which, how.ever, he has written some charming love lyrics.

Then Notês[1] on the walls who stood
    A scorn defiant flung,
And from his lips in irony
    This biting sarcasm wrung—

"We[2] speak one language, that of arms—
    We all that tongue well know;
Bid your Satrap to bring his hordes
    We'll meet him—but as foe.

And to his bond of love, we'll place
    The bullet for a seal."
Rage tore the heart of the Satrap
    Though nought his looks reveal.

But opening wide his clenchèd hand,
    Rhesitês[3] signing near,
He points to Kleisova, and says,
    "Would'st thou win honour here

I'll keep the harbour with my spears,
    Poros and Tolma's mine;[4]

[1] Nótês Botzarès.

[2] 'Ημεῖs εἴμεθα ἀγράμματοι, γλώσσαs δὲν ἐμάθαμεν, ἐμάθαμεν μόνον νὰ πολεμώμεν, was the answer given from the fort of Missolonghi; as also "*Between Greeks and Turks the only treaty is arms,*" 'Ο μεταξὺ 'Ελλήνων καὶ Τούρκων συμβιβασμόs εἶναι τὰ ὅπλα, also spoken from Missolonghi some months before the attack on Kleisova. 'Ιστορία τῆs 'Ελλήνικηs ἐπαναστάσεωs, κεφ. ΝΗ.—Trikoupis.

[3] Kiutahi, Governor of Arta.

[4] Isle of Poros.

There stands unconquered Kleisova—
  This glory shall be thine."

Biting his lip Rhesitês said,
  " Those brilliant battles won,
Were by thyself and spearmen gained
  When all the work was done—

When fire had laid brave warriors low,
  Like ashes strewn on ground ;
For never in *dead* soldiers' hands
  Were flashing falchions found.

Not mortals they—but demon foes,
  Who those mud walls defend ;
Mayhap my men may pause ere they
  With odds unseen contend.

Let be—to Kleisova I'll go
  If worsted in the fight ;
Thy spearmen let the Frenchmen lead,
  The saved we'll count at night."

At last the destined morn arrives,
  That shall the radiance shed
Of glory, and undying fame,
  Around Tsavella's head.

See, where the fleet in circle formed,
 Comes on in thick array ;
With fire and flame—in eager haste
 Kleisova low to lay.

The heavy fleet of boats bows down
 Beneath her guns' recoil,
Our island staggers, quivering ;
 From bulwarks falls the soil.

But calm and quiet save us 'neath
 That round of ceaseless fire ;
Whilst vaunting loud, Rhesitês' host
 Breathes hate and vengeful ire.[1]

With flaming rage, and furious yells,
 They strive the walls to gain ;
Four times from blood-stained flags they plant,
 The waters cleanse the stain.

Forced by our ardour, back they flee
 In wild disordered rout ;
Rhesitês from the heights beholds
 And turns his horse about.

And hotly spurring to the shore,
 He bars the vessels' ways—
And grasping climbs the foremost prow,
 And thus their landing stays.

[1] There was great jealousy between the Satrap and Kiutahi.

" Whom flee ye now, O Turks ? " he cries ;
  " Shame, shame upon you fall ;
There's not one hundred men down there
  Enclosed by yon mud wall ! "

The boats' prows turn again, the Turks
  The stubborn fight renew ;
The many slain are like a pall
  O'er those the first shots slew.

Like lightning' flashes, quick we fire,
  Our shots the shore pile high ;
When—whizzing—one blest bullet wounds
  The Vizir in the thigh.

Then follows flight more shameful still,
  Headlong the boats they seek !
Ha ! how full oft the flying balls,
  Those fleeing knees made weak !

Whilst unto God we sing our lauds,
  Pale with wan terrors they :
And thousands dead Rhesitês leaves
  In wet beds laid this day.

Mehemet's son upon the shore,
  Mid legions, mocking said—
" The *demons* conquered thee, let's see
  What *verve* our spears have bred."

Casting a burning glance to Heav'n,
 He cried, " If God thou art "——
But straight the blasphemy he stayed,
 And hid it in his heart.

Quick the well-trained Egyptian host
 Swarmed o'er the vessels' sides ;
Not tumult-rife Albanians these,
 Nor curbless Asian tribes.

The trumpets bray their thousand blasts,
 The clashing cymbals clang ;
Barbarian myriads from the shore
 On swimming horses sprang.

With slender spear and measured tread
 On come they—after each—
O'er phalanx dead, as wave on wave
 Sweeps o'er the wild sea beach.

Terrific strife !   Egyptian hosts,
 Aye—ever coming on ;
But Kleisova's unwearied swords
 To the waters sweep them down.

Death with his chilling breath of fear
 Full oft their lines disbands,
But courage ever bred anew
 Bears back the wavering bands.

'Tis the third hour of struggle waged,
  Three hours of murderous roar ;
But now will swords alone engage,
  For powder is no more.

Striking his brows the fierce Satrap
  Bids them his banner bear ;
And leaves the tents, for onslaught new
  The brazen trumpets blare—

The trumpets blare, with measured tread
  The prompt battalions pour ;
The waves they murmur 'neath their march,
  The wind gives back their roar.

Straight as one breast the many form,
  And flaming torches hold ;
It seems the day of Doom hath come
  To those that scene behold.

From the mud walls of Kleisova
  A bloody streak appears—
Th' Egyptians' lines are falling down,
  As fall the ripe wheat ears.

All 'round there surges deadlier strife,
  With hate and stubborn will,
Those Arabs, or the scorching balls
  Or cleaving falchions kill.

Tsavella then with mighty shout
   Crieth, " From walls why fight!
Forward! let swords this contest end.
   Forward! on earth alight."

Quick from the walls we spring with zeal—
   Quick flows the Arab blood ;
Trembling they cast away their spears,
   Fast flees the scatter'd brood.

No order now—in tumult wild
   Fast do the leaders flee ;
Most need no flight, for dyèd red
   Their graves lie in the sea.

A blood-stained scene of woe beholds
   That setting sun awhile ;
But the struggle ended gloriously
   For our poor barren isle.

Rhesitês leaves his thousands dead,
   The Satrap some thousands clear.
And thirty heroes we laid in earth
   The holy church [1] anear.

---

[1] Τῆς Αγίας Τριάδος, Holy Trinity.
See note on Kleisova, end of volume.
Rhesitês was most desirous to strike a decisive blow, as the Sultan had told him, "Missolonghi, or your head," ἢ τὸ Μεσολόγγι ἢ τὴν κεφαλήν σου.—TRIKOUPIS, Ἱστορία, κεφ. XII.

John Galatos.

—ALEXANDER SOUTSOS.
From Τουρχομάχον Ἑλλάδα.

JOHN GÁLATOS—his one sole child,
  A little maid scarce seven years old,
Followed him down the hillside wild,
  Fleeing a soldiery fierce and bold.
    Poor Katerina, clothed with grace,
    Fair as the cold moon's pallid face!
" Father! Father!" her shrill tones rung.
  John Gálatos still onward fled
From rock to rock, o'er chasms sprung,
  Nor stayed his feet nor turned his head.

From rock to rock, o'er chasms deep,
  The Turks behind, th' abyss below,
With one strong bound, one desperate leap,
  John Gálatos is safe from foe.
    The helpless wife, for death, remains,
    His child for slavery and chains.
He fleeth to another shore.
  His heart is wrung through eight long years:

E

"Child! child!" he crieth, "Evermore
　　Thy young voice thrilleth in my ears."

Across the Asian deserts bare,
　　To Mulasa in Karia's plain,
With one strong hope 'mid gnawing care
　　The old man seeks his child again,
　　　　Where on the hills the maiden spends
　　　　Days weary, while the goats she tends.
"The wretched girl had changed her creed
　　To please her Turkish lord," they said;
"And loss of reason was the meed
　　Divine chastisement on her laid."

She stood upon the height, and bent
　　Her gaze upon the depths below;
Her wand'ring eyes no brightness lent
　　When turning whence that cry of woe—
　　　　"My Katerina,—it is I,
　　　　My child!" "My child!" the rocks reply.
The girl with deaf ears heard his prayer;
　　As goldi'locks,[1] in fading stoop,
Two lengthy plaits of yellow hair[2]
　　Adown her pallid shoulders droop.

[1] Literally cotton-weed, Helichrysum, which is found growing
frequently on the sea-shore, and has always a tendency to droop.

[2] The frequent mention of golden hair in the Greek poets need
not appear strange. The old traditions consider the true Greek

Unmoved she stood, nor heart-glow knew,
  The stones not colder 'neath her feet ;
No meaning from his words outgrew,
  No quickened sense his pleadings greet.
    But to the unpitying Heav'n fair
    She looked, and sang her plaintive air—
" The cruel Turks they followed fast,
  My holy chrism from me tore.
The heavenly gates are barred at last,
  Alas ! I am not Christian more."

" Ah, thrice unhappy ! sing not so,
  Strong shudderings wring my wretched frame ;
I am thine only cause of woe—
  I, who now boast the father's name ! "
    He beat his breast, his hands he wrung,
    She looked upon him, and still sung—
" The cruel Turks who followed fast,
  My holy chrism from me tore.
The heavenly gates are barred at last,
  Alas ! I am not Christian more."

" My daughter ! can'st not pity yet ? "
  The old man pleadeth through his tears.

race as an auburn-haired race, and there are many fair-haired
heroes in Homer. I have myself seen many light-haired, auburn.
and even red-haired peasants.

" I am thy father—dost forget ?—
  Hath Time so changed me with the years ?
    Alas ! not Time, but Grief's strong flow
    Hath worn these furrows on my brow.
I lost thee a mere babe—again
  Thou com'st to me in woman's grace.
O bless'd old age ! my long heart-strain
  Breaks into joy at thy dear face."

Then from her eyes two sudden streams
  Of tears like fiery fountains shine ;
A thrill of passion through her gleams,
  She makes the last and holy sign,
    Then o'er the abyss herself she flings,
    And through the air her wild song rings—
" The cruel Turks who followed fast,
  My holy chrism from me tore.
The heavenly gates are barred at last,
  Alas ! I am not Christian more."

" She tore herself from my caress,"
  John Gálatos cried, " she shunned my face ;
She feared yon yawning chasm less
  Than her cursed father's fond embrace.
    Twice she would no pity show,
    Twice she spurn'd me, nor would know.

O Heav'n ! on me—on me outpour
   All—all thy wrath and vengeance dread.
Flash lightnings—loud ye thunders roar—
   On this thrice doomed and wretched head."

Our Grandmother's Girlhood.[1]

—Kostês Palamas.

.   .   .   .

"That thou art daughter mine, in sooth thyself
    must show this day."
Thus spake my father. "Through thy breast *I will*
    no terrors stray
When with a pistol in thy hand I bid thee stand
    me near,
Nor 'mid the firing lest a bullet strike thee shrink
    with fear."
So saying, 'round my neck he hung the holy wood of
    grace :
Like ruddy apples on the tree so flushed with red
    my face,

[1] In the summer of 1881 there were borne through the streets of
Athens the remains of an aged woman, in the complete costume of
a Pallikar, which dress she had worn during the terrible days of
Missolonghi, and had treasured in secret since those times. When
upon her death-bed, she referred her relatives to a chest which contained the long-cherished clothes, dear from the memories which
clung to them, and requested with her dying breath that she might
be buried in them. This fact, recorded in the daily papers of that
year, is evidently embodied in the poem from whence this extract
is taken.

As rough capote and goodly vest he clothed me
    with straightway,
When fustanella white as snow hid maiden robes
    away,
And when beneath the manly garb and fierce dis-
    play of war
I from a tender shamefast girl became a Pallikar.

He willed me at the cannon' side ever to stand him
    nigh,
With water to refresh his lips as oft as parched or dry,
To swell my cheeks that o'er his brow a breath of air
    might play,
And from his ever-dreaded blade to wash the blood
    away.
" Cosmetic [1] none, nor golden coins—but powder and
    ball I hold,"
And hear from all—" the daughter *this* of our Philios
    bold ! "

There lay before us in the field th' unnumbered
    Turkish host.
Brave were our bands and true—and well worthy this
    our boast,

---

[1] *Cosmetic* = φκιασίδι, was a rather coarse kind of rouge which appears to have been in use among the Greek as well as Turkish girls many years since. The *golden coins* = φλωριά were the many strings of florins worn around the neck as an ornament about the same time—the florin being a coin much in use before the Greek revolution.

With them my father's knowledge — my father's
    veteran skill;
And hither came his daughter night and day with
    fearless will,
Hasting amid this warring crowd, through all this
    raging flood,
Which from the deadly conflict fresh, was drunken as
    with blood.
Honour to those young warriors—to all those patriots
    true,
And the strangers, those brave Suliots, staunch
    Pallikars all through,
And mid the firing foremost aye; and ever, I aver,
Though oft in camp ill disciplined and turbulent they
    were,
Yet never, never, once from them were girl or damsel
    near
Came word that was not fitting for a modest maiden's
    ear.
But Life and Honour both for me with all their
    blessings lay —
One in my fustanella, one in the cross of grace that
    day.

Brave Philios' daughter learnt she was his very child
    in sooth !
Dear children they who knew me in those days will
    vouch this truth—

A girl with every youthful charm, trembling like leaf
    on bough,
Took a fresh life beneath the cross and seemed trans-
    formèd now.
Where maiden weapons [1] on her breast once rung with
    silver sound,
Now silver ring the manly arms, her kindling heart's
    rebound.
As though the white kilt that she wore had charmed
    her with strange pow'r,
Soon as she donned it girl was she no longer from
    that hour!
Nor think ye that I idly stood with calmly folded
    hands,
Where all my valiant brethren strove for life with
    flashing brands,
Where flew the flame wing'd bird of death the ever
    murderous shell,
Where onslaught fierce woke suddenly with ever
    murderous yell.

  .   .   .   .

As like a falcon swift I fly, what dreadful scenes are
    those
        The paths I speed disclose.

There with their closed teeth firmly set, and hungering
    as for blood,

[1] Ἅρματα. See note to Drosinês' Folk Song, "The Magic of Love."

The beardless striplings of the war in line awaiting
    stood ;
Each eye upon a gun though fixed, kindled with lively
    glow,
Nor turned aside to gaze on me as I went to and fro.
The only eyes, alas! alas! that looked upon me
    there,
Were dimm'd and agonis'd and pain'd, fill'd with a
    sad despair—
The eyes of those whose pour'd-out blood flow'd round
    them for their bed,
Who with clench'd teeth yet strove to keep the life
    which slowly fled.

Such memories not here nor now can I recall at will,
      Save with a shuddering thrill.
How was it then, and with what heart, bore I, O God,
    that life,
      With the horrors of that strife?
Maybe it was our dire despair, the manly kilt maybe,
That thus so fortified my soul, and bade pale pity flee.

  .   .   .   .

Dear children, learning, knowledge all, was judged
    in days of yore
For men alone befitting; books with all their treasured
    lore

Were not for maidens' good, said they, they learnt
  not by the book,
Lest on the written words of love their eyes might
  chance to look !
But Misery was the one school now in which we both
  were taught—
There learnt we the same lesson, and from out one
  book well-fraught
With teachings wherein other learning faded quite
  before—
Our bitter slavery 'neath the Turk, and its debase-
  ment sore ;
For male and female equal both, and teachers every-
  where,
For great and small, for young and old, around us,
  here or there,
Or in the mother's lullaby, or in the grandam's
  curse,
Or in the father's blessing, or the maiden's fears, or
  worse—
In old wives' fables—village tales—in every game or
  play,
At all our maimèd festivals enslavèd memories stay.
For ages we had heard the fiery alphabet of death,
And the Turks and demons both we exorcisèd in one
  breath.
And as the damsels for the dance would range them
  in a row,

Like unto this the murmured song which would in
    chorus flow—
"Sooner may I behold the earth with my life-blood
    dyed red,
Than e'er upon my eyelids should a Turk his kisses
    shed."

One day as I across the hill to seek my father
    went,
A dread and awful blast on high the heavens
    resounding rent;
And suddenly the mighty hosts innumerable out-
    pour—
For onslaught and for ruin spreading wide along
    the shore.
Ne'er had I heard a shout like that which tore the
    wounded air,
"The Turks! the Turks are coming on our camp,
    —prepare, prepare."
From height to height upon the wing the guns their
    lightning sped,
The crimson waters of the trench, the putrefying
    dead,
Are thrown up intermingled with the thousands
    newly slain,
Their battalion in the marauders' midst is hurlèd
    back again.

The deadly bullets as they fly, hiss as they cleave the
    air,
As though it were in mocking jest of those they
    slaughter there.

.   .   .   .

One fleeting moment I was stone, and then, with
    strong rebound,
I woke again, fresh courage took, and through the
    tempest bound ;
And like a swift-wing'd frighten'd bird, with terror
    at the strife,
I seek my nest, I seek again my father, my dear
    life.
At the Great Gun I saw him from a distance as
    I sped,
With tall and stalwart form upreared, and bare, un-
    covered head.
The Captain of the Pallikars, his swift glance fixed
    beneath ;
Around him are the showering sparks, beyond the
    fires of death.
Above his cannon towering high, holding his torch
    he stands,
That cannon he had lifted and had placed with his
    own hands.

A wide breach had been opened and our camp was
    being scaled,
The crimson flag with its one star upon the wall was
    nailed,
When promptly on the moment his loud cannon he
    uprears
As his own column wavering falls back with sudden
    fears—
" The demons are upon us, we are slain,
      O Lord Christ, help us yet again ! "

My father swift but quietly as a mother doth arise
To lay her babe i' the downy cot where unawaked it
    lies,
So with both hands embracing—what iron hands
    were those
      Which the strong cannon pose !
Then one good aim, one dread report, and to the
    Shades below,
Together with their banner, he despatched the
    murderous foe,
Hurling them backward from the breach, and as the
    routed fly,
      A mocking laugh rose high.

.   .   .   .

While laugh and scoff, re-echoing, were ringing far
    and wide,

I softly whispered " Father," as I stood by his dear
    side.
He looked on me with kindling gaze—one hand his
    torch still grasped,
And with his left, one moment more, his child he
    fondly clasped.
In the one hand there was death—in the other was
    his life,
And near him was a fair-haired youth—a nursling of
    the strife,
On me who gazed : loose streaming o'er my shoulders
    fell my hair,
My stout belt all unclasped fall'n down, left my white
    bosom bare !
He bent him o'er his gun again—mine eyes with
    shame downcast :
That youth became — well, children, well — your
    grandsire dear at last.

I love thee ! O dear garb ! in thee shine forth those
    days of old—
Honour and glory in the vest, and its cordons bright
    of gold,
Capote and fustanella, and bullets for battles'
    whirl,
The aged woman loves you with the ardour of the
    girl !

No, when the crowns of marriage[1] they were placing
    on my brow,
Such joy not even then I knew, nor such delight as
    now,
When I behold them all spread out, again before me
    laid ;
For I ne'er won such triumphs as a fair and black-
    eyed maid
With charms long fled, as then I won when under
    your control ;
With you—with you awoke the inmost feelings of
    my soul.
He loved me—him I loved full well—I found my
    husband true ;
And from drear slavery's pangs was saved through
    him alone—and you.
That night my fatherland was lost, my father,
    wounded, died ;
With you I fled unto the hills—half dead—heart-
    broke beside ;
For through my fair-haired soldier and the love that
    cloth'd me o'er,
My body was not given as a morsel for the Moor.[2]

   .   .   .   .

[1] The floral crowns worn by bride and bridegroom are *alternately* placed on the brows of each.

[2] Jousouf.

.   .   .   .

And now when drawing near I see the hour when I
    must die,
Bring forth again the raiment loved, that I may see
    it nigh.
For Charon will not seem to me so cruel and un-
    just,
If in those garments I with them resolvèd be to
    dust.

.   .   .   .

The determination of the heroic defenders of Missolonghi never
swerved.   At the last moment a message had been sent demanding
surrender.   The answer was, " Ἀποθνήσκομεν, ἀλλὰ δεν προσκυνοῦμεν "
— *We can die, but will not submit.*—Ἱστορία τῆs Ἐπαναστάσεως κεφ.
ΝΗ.

The following is one of the many *popular* songs upon the fall of
Missolonghi :—

    " Ποιὸs θὲ ν' ἀκόυση κλάμματα, γυνάικα μυρολόγια
      Διαϐὰτ' ἀπὸ τὸ Κάραλο, κι ἀπὸ το Μεσολόγγι
      Κ'ἐκεῖ ν'ἀκοῦστε κλάμματα, ἀνδρὶκια μυρολόγια
      Πῶs κλαῖν' μαννάδες γιὰ παιδιά, καὶ τὰ παιδιὰ γιὰ μάνναις.
      Δὲν κλαῖνε γιὰ τὸ σκοτομό, ποῦ θὲ νὰ σκοτωθοῦνε
      Μὸν' κλαῖνε γιὰ τὸ σκλαβωμό, ποῦ θὲ νὰ σκλαβωθοῦνε."

He who would listen to lamentations and the wailing of women,
let him go to Karolo and Missolonghi : there will he hear mourning
and loud myriologies—mothers weeping for their children, children
for their mothers.   They weep not for the slaughter of those who
are slain—they weep for the slavery of those who are made slaves.
—Ἀνθολογία ὑπὸ Ν. Μικαλοπόυλου. Σελ 118.

The Rock and the Wave.[1]

—Aristotle Valaôritès.

" FALL back, thou Rock, and let me pass !" thus spake
   th' embolden'd Wave
To the crag by the hollow shore which the strong
   and lashing waters lave.
" Fall back, against my breast thou'st lain long while
   full hard and cold,
Whilst the north wind nestled in thee and the fierce
   wild tempest rolled.
Light sands are not the arms I bear, nor empty hollow
   moans,
But a stream with blood bestainèd red which hath
   broadened with my groans !
The curse of the world is with me, the world which
   'pressed me sore—

[1] This poem, called an allegory by the poet, was written for, and
dedicated to, the political guild at Corfu, named the Regeneration,
'Η 'Αναγέννησις, in 1863, in order to celebrate the 42d anniversary
of the day of the Rising, March 25, 1821. In it are expressed all
those hopes and beliefs in his country's future greatness which are
the leading features in the writings of Valaôritès.

The world which crieth now to thee: 'Fall, rock—
    thy day is o'er.'
I came to thee in silence—creeping—trembling—and
    afraid—
A slave! but at thy feet I dug, and deadly hollows
    made.
Thou looked'st on me with mocking scorn, in jest
    thou bad'st the world
Laugh at the frothy foam by light winds tossed aloft
    and whirled;
But where I seemed to kiss thee, there—in secret—
    night and day,
I ate into thy body, and I gnawed thy flesh away.
The deep wound which I opened, and the lake cut
    by my hands,
I covered them with sea-weed, and I hid them in the
    sands.
Bend down and see thy roots that once struck deep
    below the sea,
Thou'rt but a hollow pebble, and 'tis I who've wasted
    thee.
Fall back, thou Rock, and let me pass, the feet of
    thy poor slave
Shall tread upon thy neck—I wake as a lion from
    my grave."

The Rock in stupor sleepeth on, whilst hidden there
    it seems

F *

As 'twere the winding sheet of Death which through
    the cold mist gleams.
The pale moon casts her half-quenched rays upon his
    wrinkled brow,
And shows the jagged rents. The curse of ages
    sweepeth now
Across his dreams, while dismal shapes within the
    whirlwind meet,
And flapping wings of birds unclean who Death's
    foul odours greet.

A thousand times the Rock had heard the murmur
    of the Wave,
A thousand times had heard unmoved the fearful
    threats she gave;
But now, to-day arousing, he doth shudder while he
    pleads—

" What would'st thou, Wave, from me ? why dost
    thou threaten, what thy needs?
Who art thou that thus darest ? who instead of cool-
    ing streams—
Instead of song from ripplings sweet—to lull me in
    my dreams,
Dost stand erect before me, crowned with foam and
    rearing high—
Who, and whate'er thou art—learn this—not easily
    I die ! "

"Rock! 'tis *Revenge!* the cup the Ages made me drink was scorn,
The dregs were bitter, but I grew beneath the anguish borne:
Once I was but a tear, look on me now, behold and see—
An Ocean have I grown into, fall down and worship me.
That is not drifting weed thou see'st wide spreading o'er my breast,
But hosts of living souls, and strong in angry just unrest—
The curses of the Hell thou didst create, awake *thee* now.
Thou mad'st of me a grave, and thy burthens weighed me low,
Thou dravest me to other shores; my tears—and my soul's strife—
Were but a scoff, whilst alms and doles were poisoning my heart's life.
Fall back, thou Rock, and let me pass—my quiet calm onflow
Shall swallow thee and pass along—*I, thy remorseless foe.*"

The Rock was mute—the Wave arose in wrath and swept along—

The hollowed Rock gives way, engulfed within the
    current strong.
It is lost in the Abyss.   For awhile the angered sea
Rages above, but soon in peace roams onward broad
    and free.
And where a wall of stone once stood there now a
    harmless wave
Sporteth in playful rippling above the hard Rock's
    grave.

IDYLLS AND ODES.

The Slave.

—Aristotle Valaôrités.

Open wide your pinions
  Faithful, tender dove,
And to the far-off battle-field
  Haste thee hence for love.
The way is long before thee,
  And thou must fly alone;
Spread—spread thy plumèd winglets,
  And speed thee—speed thee on.

And when thou go'st through cloudland,
  As thou dost cleave the air,
And comest where the lightnings
  Are sitting brooding there—
Ah! then, dear dove, bethink thee,
  Or burnt may be the thread
Which ties the words I've written;
  Would then that I were dead!

And when thou see'st the billows
  With foamy crest uprear,

Upon the far shore dashing
 As though to bring it fear—
Bird, do not thou then linger,
 Nor near the breakers stay,
For those deceiving waters
 Would wash my words away.

The waves are ever pitiless—
 For water thirsting still,
And they would rise above thee
 To drink their greedy fill
Of the tears which now are standing
 On the letter thou dost bear:
Ah! may I die! if *he* see not
 The words I've written there.

And if, along thy pathway
 Through ether far away—
O faithful dovelet of my heart!
 Upon some fair spring day
The sad and joyless swallows
 It chanceth thee to meet,
Give them this kiss in loving,
 And their dear coming greet;

And tell them my heart' sorrow,
 And how in piteous truth,

In the harem of a Moslem
  Doth fade and pale my youth;
And bid them near my window
  Not to forget to rest,
But straightway come, and near me
  Build up one little nest.

But if, when thou shalt meet them,
  Thou findest them dismay'd,
Pursued of churlish winter,
  And sadden'd and afraid;
Remember, dove, thy pinions
  To preen again with care,
And lift thy wings before thee
  Like a boat' sails spreading fair.

While thus ye voyage together,
  Thou shalt in whispers low
Confide to them each secret
  That weights thy heart with woe.
Those swallows, dove, remember
  To tell them as ye fly,
That two long years are number'd
  In slavery whilst I lie.

And there, when first arriving,
  In their first tumult gay,

Bid them beseech my brothers
   To bear me hence away;
And ever in the dawning
   Remind them in their song,
How, in this land of Turkey,
   I'm weary, waiting long.

But thou, my dovelet, speeding,
   Still onward, onward fly,
To where the Klephts are holding
   Agrapha's[1] mountain high;
And seek my Life—my Lambro,
   My love who aye shall be,
And give this kiss in secret,
   With these fond words from me.

And pray him with this greeting,
   That I be ne'er forsook,
For I am fresh and lovely
   As the waters of the brook;
And say how I'm endangered,
   How tyrannised my state,
But say—that for a glance of mine
   How thousands still await.

And if he of my girlhood
   Some mem'ry yet doth keep,

[1] The stronghold of the Klephts.

If sometimes while he dreameth
  He sees me in his sleep,
Oh bid him hasten hither,
  And high his falchion wave—
For poor Arêty trembleth,
  And liveth, still a slave.

If some had pluck'd his violets,
  And their sweet scent inhaled,
If they'd breathed upon my roses,
  And they had drooped and paled—
Less sorrow had it brought me,
  Nor had he made such moan ;
Ah, youth, soon, soon it withers
  In slavery drear and lone !

The Bell.—(ΤΟ ΣΗΜΑΝΤΡΟΝ.[1])

—Aristotle Valaórités.

Blow! blow! O north wind, blow!
  And filled sails speed;
Blow! blow!   Upon my oars
  My hands they bleed,
  My fingers scorch,
The row-locks burn beneath.
  Parched are my lips,
And spent my fainting breath.

[1] The word "Σήμαντρον" would be more correctly rendered by "signal" rather than "bell," but the former word would not convey to the mind the meaning required. The "Σήμαντρον" is merely a flat slab of wood, and is struck by iron or wooden hammers. It was substituted for the Κώδων—the proper metallic bell, after the conquest of Constantinople by the Turks; because the Κώδων was considered to be expressive of insolence, "nimiam securitatem," as Angelo Roccha in his commentary upon bells expresses it. The first Σήμαντρον is stated to have been made from fragments of the great bell of St. Irene, when it was broken up. The first Κώδων had been a present from Burgundy to the Byzantine Emperor, A.D. 872, after which its use became general all over Greece. Durant quaintly shows the dislike to bells to be shared equally by *Turks* and *demons*. See Appendix Notes.

Other water have I none, O sea, but thine—
With thine I wet my mouth, but bitter is thy brine.

A sea which hath no wave,
On the shore to burst,
Seemeth like two sweet eyes
For tears athirst.
Or a throbless heart,
Or hopes which ever lose,
Nights with no dawn,
Nor rain of fresh'ning dews.
Love without dreaming, Pindus void of snows,
Or wingless bird, or nightingale which ever songless
goes.

Blow! blow! and to my love
Bear me once more;
She is ill—lest she should die
Doth fret me sore;
Can a cloud be lost
E'er hath been lost a wave,
To a heart that loves
Could the world become a grave!
Ye are mute—ye scarcely breathe—O hills! O valleys
dear!
Good wind! north wind! have pity—my father, O
north wind, hear!

> Lingering with me last night
> . The beach along,
> My mother clasped my head
> With feeling strong,
> Sweet was the kiss
> She gave me as she blest,
> And bade me soon
> Come back to her lone breast ;

O wind ! north wind ! my mother for me doth sigh :
She is old, if she see me not, alas ! she will surely
   die.

Once more his wearied trembling hands he moistens,
   once again
They grasp the oars which strike upon and beat the
   sullen main.
'T would seem as though the sorrows which his hapless
   bosom steep,
Lift up the sailor's oars on high and plunge them in
   the deep.
The north wind listens not to him, neither the dark
   sea-wave,
And still the stretched-out ocean lies like marble o'er
   a grave.
The sailor looketh on his boat which rests on her sea-
   bed
Like to a pleasant dream which oft o'er tranquil
   sleep is shed ;

Nor dares he stir, nor dareth he to sleep lest chance
  it may
That her shadow make the sails its wings, and flee
  —yea, fly away.

Beautiful was the widowed Night—a widow though
  newly wed,
Who longeth for her beloved one—by Fate returning
  led.
How many are th' enamoured eyes which her afresh
  behold,
And she remaineth all unmoved, with hands which
  clasping fold.
The Heaven for her adorning his myriad stars doth
  bring,
And unto her he holdeth out the moonbeams for a
  ring :
He offers her a thousand clouds, he offers flow'rs
  and dews,
And she remaineth silent still, nor once the heaven
  views.
The plane-tree his green glorious boughs before her
  spreadeth wide,
And the hands of the deep black cypress stretch forth
  unto her side, '
As though they were desiring the lovely Night
  t' embrace,

G

And longing with their fingers her dark hair to inter-
 lace.
And she remaineth silent still, she looketh for the sun—
The golden sun so wholly fair, who love for her hath
 none.
She turns her eyes unto the hills—to the woods—and
 to the shore,
To see if that bright shining one will not return once
 more.
And yonder on the sea instead, the black-eyed
 nymph sees now
The sailor who is mourning—lonely sitting on the
 prow.
No longer lifteth he the oars; his boat moves not,
 whilst he,
Turning away, awaiteth mute the hand of Destiny.

Often, full oft adown his face the tears which rolling
 flow
One after other fall upon the lifeless sea below—
Those tears the dark deep swalloweth ; but should a
 tempest come,
And shake with strength the sleeping wave, whit'ning
 the shores with foam,
Who knoweth where those tears will fall, who knows
 but where *she* stands—

The mother, waiting his return will find them on the
    sands.

The Night beholds him 'plaining, and she openeth
    her wings,
And then around him silently her peaceful arms she
    flings;
She softly clasps him unto her, and raineth on him
    dews,
And wipeth off with fingers light the tears his eyes
    suffuse.
His youth's fond dreams she layeth as a pillow for his
    head,
And secret balmy breathing hopes she streweth for
    his bed.
Then as he sinks in slumber sweet her lips they
    softly stoop,
And kisses lay upon his lids which yet half open
    droop
And quiver as the dove's soft wings that tremble o'er
    her breast,
When secretly she spreadeth them to brood upon her
    nest.
And thereupon the sailor dreams that his own love
    draws near,
Who comes to seek him, bringing him a kiss, and
    finds him here;

And he smileth sweetly in his sleep, as doth the
    suckling smile,
Believing that its mother's breast its lips still press
    the while.
The Night that smile beholding, deep joy her heart
    possessed,
And she took it for adorning, and wore it on her
    breast;
And then she rose up silently, nor would she break
    his rest,
But gracefully she moves away to hide her in the
    West.
And still at every step she takes she turneth back
    her head,
To look upon the sailor whom she leaves in that lone
    bed.

And thus at last the dawning breaks, when through
    the woods are heard
The chanting of the shepherds, and the chirping of
    the bird;
The husbandman [1] his two good oxen yoketh with all
    speed,

---

[1] Mons. Pouqueville, in his "Voyage de la Grèce," gives a similar
picture, with one exception, "Au point du jour le paysan grec prend
son hoyau, fait le signe de la croix ; et chargeant ses instruments
aratoires *sur les epaules de sa femme,* précédé de ses bœufs, il se
rend au champ," Liv. iv. chap. vii. It would seem now that the
seed-bag, &c., are carried upon the shoulders best calculated to bear

And with the goad·just pricking them, straight to
    his field doth lead,
He cries—"Come, Bee; come, Beauty," and laden
    with his plow,
With his seed-store on his shoulders, thrice happy is
    he now!
The herdsman much rejoicing like a gazelle doth
    spring,
Casteth a morsel to his dog, and forth his flock doth
    bring.
Deep drinking of the foaming milk, wherewith his
    cup he fills,
He bids his sheep to follow him, and goeth to the
    hills.[1]
Then waking—to the heavens high the starling flies
    away,[2]
That it may meet in gladsomeness the morn's first
    op'ning ray.

them, from the general demeanour of the women, as seen by a
recent visitor among rustic scenes. "All the faces are bright, songs
and laughter resound everywhere, and above all rise the shrill
exhortations and reprimands of the women to disobedient or tired
oxen, every one of whom has its own name (as in the poem), derived
generally from its colour. Hence the appellations often sound
strange, as "Hey, Black Eyes;" "Go within, White Lips;"
"Here, Dove," &c. Ἀγρότικαι ἐπιστολαι ὑπὸ Γεοργίου Δροσίνη.

[1] Nothing ever appealed more to my feelings than the picturesque
scene of these dark-browed shepherds preceding their numerous
flocks over the hills, and cheering them on with voice and gesture.

[2] "Innumerable flocks of starlings arrive in Greece in April."
POUQUEVILLE, *Voyage de la Grèce.*

The doleful mother waketh too, who prays her son's
    return,
And calling on Our Lady's name, doth to the ingle
    turn ;
With withered fingers wipes away the tear-drops
    from her eyes,
And lights again the quenchèd fire : anew the sparks
    arise.
And the world recalled to busy life waketh to care
    again—
Sorrow and Hope together wake—joy, poverty, and
    pain.

And 'mid this fresh tumultuous life which o'er all
    Nature breaks,
The wave of the shore awaketh, and the little vessel
    takes ;
The currents draw it on and on, whilst for one
    moment more
A strong wind bloweth lustily to waft it to the shore ;
And still the sailor sleeping lies as the bark is skim-
    ming on,
As though some secret mystic hand were urging it
    along.

A bell through the silence boometh, it sounds a
    funereal knell,

"Clang! clang! what meaning hath it—whose death
        hath it come to tell?
The valley it doth re-echo it—clang! clang! it moans
        again,
And the wind that is carrying it hath fear for that
        sorrowful refrain.

Spell-bound the boat stays motionless, her sails flap
        with unrest,
Her masts are creaking, and her cords hang quiver-
        ing on her breast;
The stream stirs not, as though 'twere changed to
        marble it doth lie,
And still clang! clang! booms the passing bell—who
        hath now come to die!

The heart of the sailor lying there is troubled in his
        sleep,
The whilst before him in a dream bright hopes and
        gladness sweep;
His lids are wide distended—wildly his eyes they
        roll:
What tones were those he seemed to hear that with
        tremor fill his soul?
But hushed is the bell in silence now, all still—none
        other sound—
None other than his own heart-throbs, which beat
        with strong rebound.

Was it a cruel dream, and flown as a bird away doth
    fly;
Or did he shiver in the chill of a zephyr passing by.
Which from the mouth of the dawning came and
    ere 't would wake him there,
Had softly breathed in sportiveness among his auburn
    hair?

Now comes the wished-for shore in view, and now
    the heights appear,
And from afar the village-cots are showing white and
    clear.
The sailor with a clutching hand graspeth his oars
    anew,
And swiftly again they are gliding his manly fingers
    through.
The sea is cut in furrows as behind him foam-clouds
    fly,
Whilst he upon those village-homes doth fix a stead-
    fast eye:
He gazeth on the smoke-cloud that is rising from
    each roof
Thick, black, and dense—he breathes again, hope
    comes for his behoof;
And in the blindness of his joy one roof he seeth
    not,
From whence no smoke is issuing—he noteth not
    that cot,

The which alone is keeping its two windows closèd
    fast,
As if indeed the hand of Death had o'er its eyelids
    past.

The sailor hath sped, hath swiftly sped, his boat hath
    flown as the wind ;
But yet he believeth ever it hath slowly lagged
    behind :
Deeply the oars he plungeth down, 'neath his strong
    hands they bound,
They are grating within the row-locks, and the
    splinters fly around.
The sailor he nothing feareth—at once to his feet he
    springs,
And quickly into the ocean's midst, baring himself,
    he flings.
His hands and his arms are measuring the wide waters
    which he beats,
And his ample chest is dispersing far the thousand
    foams it meets.

The waves unto the swimmer are a hope and a delight :
As though he were a dolphin he goes through them
    in his might ;
And many thousand thoughts are those that rush into
    his mind.

As though it were the last last time they could an
    entrance find.
And he thinks upon his cottage home, remembering
    the day
When with his mother he a youthful stripling went
    that way.
They went together through the storm—through the
    black tempest's roar ;
To seek and find his father dear they went unto that
    shore.
He remembers how they called him by his name the
    whole night through,
He remembers how upon the sands their necks they
    crouched low,
Before a wave which frenzied came as to the shore
    'twas borne,
And brought with it that corpse beloved, sea buffeted
    and torn.
He remembers how they buried him close to yon
    cypress tree,
Which near the lonely little church afar he now can
    see.
He remembers when they hollowed out and heaped
    again the earth
Above, where the dear body of his father lay
    beneath—
That near unto him weeping stood a gentle maiden
    there

(And she too was an orphan), sprightly, innocent, and
    fair.
From childhood they had loved, and now above the
    father's grave
They were betroth'd, and fond embrace his mother,
    blessing, gave.
He remembers that belovèd one—that mother calls to
    mind—
And griefs, and joys, and dreams within his heart
    their birthplace find
Like frothy foam which ever crowns the crest of our
    youth's wave,
And quenched in vapour melts away like incense
    o'er a grave.

Death Ode.

In the dawning 'mid the dewing a rose was blooming
    gay,
In the dawning mid the dewing the rose had paled
    away.
A nightingale 'mong its green boughs right joyfully
    did sing,
And built therein a little nest for this one gladsome
    spring;
The spring will come again, and the bird in loving
    quest,
        But where—but where the nest?

When the moon led out her shining train with all
    the starry bands,
They looked on it with longings deep, and stretch-
    ing forth their hands,
As though they wished it with them in their own
    bright home above,
They said that it was one of them—the sister of
    their love,

Who, wandering through the heavens and alone, had
  missed its way.
O stars! O stars! too soon, alas! you've called it
  hence away.

There were who heard the nightingale which sang
  the boughs among,
Might say, "No lay of gladness this, but a funereal
  song."
There were who saw the glistening rays which had
  the heavens left
To glint upon and shimmer through the leaves of the
  bereft,
Could say, "These are not gladsome lights, nor
  shining lamps of joy,
But tapers which in funeral trains the mourners'
  hands employ."

In the dawning 'mid the dewing a rose was blooming
  gay,
In the dawning 'mid the dewing the rose had paled
  away.
Had the north wind passed along, and with chilling
  blast been there,
And, cruel lover, looking on that rose so fresh and
  fair,
        Made its sweetnesses his prey,
        And bore them on his wings away?

So withered now, so wan its leaves, you'd say long
  time the morn
Had passed it by, nor given dews to freshen and
  adorn ;
Or one might say 'twas like a bloom that doth un-
  timely fade,
Which on a silent shrouded form some loving hand
  hath laid.
  A grace and charm to shed
  Around the dear one dead.

In the dawning 'mid the dewing a rose was blooming
  gay,
In the dawning 'mid the dewing the rose had paled
  away.

I know not, but one saith indeed that yesternight
  and late,
A form was seen which swept along like smoke by
  breezes blown.
And black his horse as midnight deep, or dark as
  darkest Fate,
  And light as zephyrs flown.
He held a pale rose in his hand, which to a bare
  stalk clung,
And as he sped along the heights no tear from him
  was wrung.

He only said to the waves that saw him and shrunk
  away,
    " 'Tell me, O wavelets, tell,
Is not this rose most lovely ? "   To the grass which
  dying lay,
    Where the hoofs of his courser fell,
" Say, am not I then worthy, am I not fit to wear
    A rose so fresh and fair ?
Is not Death's breast made beautiful by flowers with
  such hue ? "
    Alas ! too true, too true !

All Souls' Day.[1]

Within thy shadowy depths, O cypress drear,
I' the midnight hour will come and linger near
A father, who has lost his daughter fair;
And night and day he wand'reth ev'rywhere,
But seeketh her in vain. All whom he asketh, say
They have not seen her pass, and weeping turn
    away.

'Neath the moonbeams yester eve
    He sought her cherish'd tree,
And prayed it of the lov'd one
    Who came to gather free
Of its roses for adorning,
    When to holy church she'd go;
And it answered soft and low—

[1] When writing this poem, and the Death Ode, it is probable that the poet had in his mind his daughter Maria, concerning whose recent death he says, in the dedication to the vol. Μνημόσυνα, addressed to his friend Emilius Typaldos, "I feel pressing upon my breast all the earth I threw over my beloved Maria." Ποιήματα Ἀριστοτέλους Βαλαωρίτου.

" I saw her every morning,[1]
    And like myself, most fair !
My roses she would number—
    Were one missing there
She would chide me, and would say,
' Although great the love she bore,
She'd forsake me evermore.'

But she'd pluck, tho' blaming,
    My dew-besprinkled flow'rs,
And deck her snowy bosom,
    Shedding scented showers ;
All who saw her then would say,
Looking on my blushful hue,
' She's in sooth thy sister true.'

Tell me, tell me, Father,
    Lest she angered be,
Hath she bid thee hither
    To say she comes to me ?
Three days have I awaited
From her rosy mouth a kiss,
And still her dear presence miss."

---

[1] " Dans l'ancienne littérature, pour l'instinct gréc, l'homme n'est pas un être isolé au milieu de la nature inanimée et des autres êtres,—tout est doué de la vie,—des arbres, les rivières, les montagnes, les parents defunts sont toujours à venir apporter secours ou conseil aux membres survivants de la famille. La même croyance, ou plutôt la même foi, s'observe dans toute l'école Epirote."—LAMBER, *Grecs Contemporains.*

He goeth to the night flow'r,
　　He sees it pal'd away :
" Flow'r," he saith, " what aileth thee,
　　Thy colours why so grey ?
Yester eve for thy refreshing
Did my Mary fail to bring
Cooling waters from the spring ? "

" In the night's most solemn hour
　　With waking lids I wait,
Hoping Mary still would seek me
　　Coming as of late,
When methought I saw her stand
Close within a moonlight ray,
And with the moonbeam flit away."

And thus while low it whisper'd, a voice was heard
　　anear,
And these the words in mournful tones that met the
　　father's ear—

" I saw her borne along by four,
　　With flowers o'er her strown,
In every eye that saw her pass
　　Were tears of pity shown ;
The Holy Cross on high before,
Priests behind—in order meet,
Lighted tapers—incense sweet.

Yes ! I saw your Mary stretch'd
    Upon her wooden bier ;
But seek her not within the church,
    Her grave thou'lt find is near,
Where the smoke of incense now,
Curling round, ascendeth high
From the earth where she doth lie.

If thou longest her to meet,
    There is dawning festal great,
When to-night the dead rejoice,
    Going as in bridal state
From their tombs in sereclothes white,
To taste the holy cakes [1] so fair,
That hands of loving friends prepare.

When the midnight draweth near,
    And the birds to chirp begin,
Come thou then, and mourn alone,
    Close the cypress shade within.
Then as All Souls' day is here,
To thine arms she'll come once more,
Asking kisses as before."

---

[1] Κόλυβα, cakes of remembrance made of boiled corn, and offered on the day of burial, All Souls' Day, and the anniversary of death, first blessed in the church and then distributed to friends, relations, and also given away to the poor in the streets. The custom is of ancient derivation. These wheaten cakes are also given away in the churches on the first Saturday in Lent.

Behind the Sanctuary there
  To wait and watch he went.
And when boom'd forth the midnight hour,
  The tomb its covering rent;
And his Mary, clad in white,
Gliding to his loving breast,
On his lips her kisses prest.

" Sweetest Father," saith she then,
  " Thou seest I am cold;
If 'tis true thou lovest still
  Thy Mary as of old,
Come and share my tomb with me,
For the darkness doth me 'fright
All alone in Hades' night.

See the winding sheet is wide,
  'Twill cover us full well;
Let us hence, for soon, behold,
  Skies will dawning tell.
I am trembling and a-chill,
For I'm but a fragile thing,
Lonely left and sorrowing.

.   .   .   .

.   .   .   .

Behold, what dainty bed is here!
  They took from out my hair,

The roses which from mine own tree
    I'd plucked and twinèd there,
And now they widely scattered lie
All o'er my winding sheet below,
Which shineth white as purest snow?"

There, while he clasped her warmly—there, whilst
    her lips he kissed,
She glideth from his fond embrace, and passeth as a
    mist.
The bird doth sing the dawning, and dazzling breaks
    the day—
Mourn for the lovely maiden—for the father mourn
    alway.

The Two Angels.

—Julius Typaldos.

With black and outspread wings,
By Night's o'ershadow'd breast,
The Angel of Death went forth
Out of the veilèd West.
At his onward flight the winds,
The rippling brooks were stilled;
And the silence of the grave
At once all Nature filled.

The Angel, lo, of Life
Flew from the other side,
And fragrant scents untold
In his path he scatter'd wide;
The stars above rained down
A sweet mysterious light,
And from the earth sprang forth
Green grass, and flowers bright.

And midway in the heav'ns
Met there the angels twain,

When earth, and sea, and stars
Paused tremblingly again—
As by the Last-day's summons
They had surprisèd been,
When they saw thus paired together
Life and the dread unseen.

ANGEL OF LIFE.

" Restrain thee—oh restrain
　　Thy pinions' darksome flight ;
　　How many gleaming joys
　　Before them quench in night !

ANGEL OF DEATH.

" How many too the sorrows
　　That oft my hands resolve,
　　When o'er the joyless mortal
　　The clouded years revolve."

Still onward through high ether,
　　Go the Angels side by side ;
　　When from on high beholding
　　A girl in beauty's pride—

Who with all tender graces,
　　Mid all her youthful charms,

Shall be borne off whilst resting
 In her loved bridegroom's arms.

At once they down descending,
 With wings that swiftly move,
 Unseen—the twain together
 Enter the shrine of love.

The scented bridal garments
 Lie scattered all around,
 And in the chamber hanging
 Two bridal wreaths are found.

ANGEL OF DEATH.

" Thou art sleeping, fair one,
 In thy loved one's arms,
 But warm hearts grow colder,
 Fading youthful charms ;
 Whilst thy breast encloseth
 Paradise—depart
 Whilst for thee—enkindled,
 Throbs another heart."

ANGEL OF LIFE.

" Brother—of her beauty
 Wilt thou not have ruth ? "

Angel of Death.

" The guileless soul e'erliving
  Breaks her mortal chain ;
  Pure and clothed for heaven
  Seeks her God again,
  Where shall ne'er be quenchèd,
  Or loveliness or youth."

Three days have hardly glided,
  Three days scarce sped along,
  Since from that door outpassing
  With gladsomeness and song,

A fair girl much belovèd,
  A comely youth beside ;
  And in each breast a heaven
  Of blissful hopes that hide.

And now from that same portal
  With bridal robes o'erspread ;
  The same fair girl—Oh, hapless !
  Goes out—but borne forth dead.

Together back through ether
  Flew then the angels twain,
  And there rose as they went onward,
  Singing, and sorrow's plain.

Hardly the Day hath shinèd,
  Ere 'tis by Night surprised ;
The rose in the earth decaying
Whence fair it sprung so prized.

Sorrow and Joy unwearied
  Betwixt them a chaplet weave,
  Which round the brows of mortals
  An unknown hand doth wreathe.
  One hastens on and striveth
  Joy to secure and bind ;
  But who flieth ever forward
  The other alone will find.

The Child and Death.

A CHILD as fair as a flow'r of May,
Sits on a river's bank one day,
And throws red blossoms in its tide,
To see them o'er the wavelets glide.

Like lightning gleams in the waters fair,
The perfum'd locks of its golden hair,
But still unchanged the waters flow,
And, tossed aside, the roses throw.

CHILD.

"O graceless river! thy banks carest,
Are all with roses and myrtles drest;
Yet thou thy waves fling'st evermore,
O graceless stream! to a far-off shore:

Whilst I all bliss and gladness find
Within my mother's arms confined."

A wave from the other side now strove
To seize the flower thrown from above,
When from amid the waters bright,
Arose an old man—hoary, white ;
The child it gazed on his silver beard,
But looked in his face and straightway feared.

Death.

" Why sitt'st thou, O little one, lonely here ? "

Child.

" I await my mother, who draweth near."

Death.

" Within these arms my darling come,
I've looked for thee to share my home."

Child.

"Thy garments and form are moist and cold.
Chilled are all those thine arms enfold."

Death.

" I've strown the flowers thou'st given me
All o'er me lest cold should reach to thee.

Never on earth before my eyes
An angel like to thee did rise.

Come to my place, there are gems in store,
Pastimes, and songs ne'er heard before."

CHILD.

" How will my mother's heart be torn
When seeking,—she'll find herself forlorn ! "

DEATH.

" Thy mother knoweth my home full well,
And seeking, will find thee where I dwell ;
Where thou liest in my arms, she'll wend her
    way
Thither at dawning and close of day."

CHILD.

" White robes and a flower-coronal
She prepareth for Christmas festival."

DEATH.

" To the church, all clothed in shining white,
She will bear thee like an angel bright."

CHILD.

" Old man, my mother upon her breast
Sings me with sweet lullabies to rest."

Death.

" Thou on my breast all hush'd will keep,
And without dreaming ever sleep."

Child.

" At night my mother will lie awake,
And longing for me her heart will break."

Death.

" Throughout the night all still and lone,
So soft, dear babe, I'll lay thee down,
That in her loving arms 'twill seem
She clasps thee in a happy dream."

Child.

" The flower I tend at break of day
Unwater'd will wither and droop away."

Death.

" For thee are blooms of thousand hues,
And night-stars on them shed their dews."

Child.

" Pale is thy face, thy glance is drear,
Old man, I look on thee and fear."

DEATH.

" Thou'lt shed o'er me so bright a ray,
'Twill chase the dark mists all away."

CHILD.

" I hear my mother's wailing cry."

DEATH.

" The wind amid the boughs doth sigh."

CHILD.

" What stifling sobs the winds repeat!"

DEATH.

" The murmuring waves the hard rocks beat."

CHILD.

" Mother, I'm here with sleep opprest,
Let me now lie upon thy breast."

DEATH.

" Behold this flower entwoven bed,
·What perfumes sweet the earth doth shed!

Now lie thee down dear child, the kiss
Thy mother brings thou shalt not miss,

When black night cometh all in shade,
To earth down droop'd, a flower doth fade."

CHILD.

" The lake hath quench'd the sunbeams bright,
A thousand colours flash with light."

DEATH.

" A new quench'd ray resembleth there
A golden bird which cleaves the air."

CHILD.

" Sweetest kisses around me play
And unknown songs "——

DEATH.

" It hath passed away."

CHORUS (on high).

" O Earth, O Stars, ring forth and say
· The Saviour—He is born this day.' "

ONE VOICE.

"Awhile, O Angel, stay the song divine,
One other little seraph comes to join its voice to thine."

And now the joyless mother draweth near
To seek her darling—and she finds it here
Like a lily lying in a flower-bed—
And kisses it while trembling—*it is dead.*

Easter=tide.

—Elias Tantalidés.

" Μύρισ' ἡ δάφνη's τοὺς ναούς, Χριστὸς ἀνέστη ψάλλουν·"

In the church there is perfume of bay.[1]—" Christ is
    arisen " they sing ;
A song of joy thou too, my love, wilt thou not from
    thy heart's gladness bring—
        See'st thou the dance ? see'st thou the kiss ?
        Easter-tide aye bringeth bliss.
The flowers of Spring they are placing on every
    brow—
        Let thine own be crownèd now !

" Christ is arisen " they sing, I will see if thou'lt
    now say me nay,
Or if as a Christian thou'lt give the triple embrace
    of to-day. .

[1] The boughs of the bay tree are universally used for church
decoration on Easter Sunday, and also as a substitute for palm on
Palm Sunday.

What! wilt thou the kiss deny?
Little coquette! stay, stay, O fie!
My fond soul is pleading while standing beside my
    lips' gates
      Thy rosy mouth where it awaits.

List the voices, and see the gay smiles when children
    and strangers now meet,
As within the church-porch all around they with
    kisses each lovingly greet;
      If *thou* Easter passest o'er
      Christian art thou now no more.
So long have I fasted for thee, that standing before
    thee again
      I am quivering in every vein.

The crimson eggs[1] hither bring quickly; come, let
    us strike them, and see
If thou art conquered—a kiss in thy cheeks' laughing
    dimples for me!

[1] This refers to a custom among children, especially popular among boys, where one holds a red Easter egg with the top uppermost, and another holding one the reverse way strikes that beneath, and he whose egg is cracked or broken forfeits it to the striker. Here the forfeit was a kiss. The day preceding Easter piles of these red eggs are exhibited in all places for sale, and are seen in course of preparation in every homestead; after Easter is well ushered in, the ground is literally strewn with fragments of red shells.

  Place thine egg mine own below—
  'Tis broken—I'm the victor now :
Ha, ha! in no-wise indeed will we break our agree-
  ment in this,
   So give me—give to me my kiss.

Lenoula.

—Demetrius Bikélas.[1]

" Lenoula ! see'st thou not I've donned my gala garb
  to-day,
My gold-embroider'd camisole, my silken sash so
  fine !
My crimson shoes—what comeliness ! what goodly
  grace is mine !
Do I not look as though to bridal feast I'd haste
  away ?
Ah ! when will God so honour me that I thine own
  may see !
Why dost thou blush ? Is it for fear lest thou a
  nun become,

[1] Mr. Bikélas has not devoted himself for some years to writing poetry; it has been of late, as the accomplished translator of Shakespeare into his native tongue, that he has been more generally known—an undertaking in which his admirable rendering can hardly be too highly spoken of. In France, Italy, and Germany he is held in the greatest estimation for his varied literary gifts.

I *

Or suitors none presenting, stay husbandless at
    home;
Or dost thou think that beauty, wit, is lacking unto
    thee?

Thou'rt fair, a maid of noble birth, and well endowed
    with mind,
And a good, right worthy husband, my Lenoula, I
    shall find.
Who knows! maybe in Lárissa to-day I'll meet with
    one,
And I who go alone this morn may bring me back a
    son—
A son-in-law of station high, with curled fair hair
    and tall.
Why dost thou turn away thy head? What doth
    that blush recall?

Ho! Pallikars! away—away, the sun declineth
    now,
Our restless horses paw the ground in our court-yard
    below;
Away—I will to Lárissa ere darkness doth us
    find,
Where lovely eyes will look at us the *jalousies*
    behind.

The Turks with low salaams will greet when meeting
    on the way,
And the mother 'll tell her child, and the old man
    tell his son,
How Lambro Krabariti into Lárissa rode on—
With ten brave lads—ten Pallikars, in brave and rich
    array !
The Pasha too will behold us boys, and see what
    soldiers bold
Those wolves are which our gorges and untrodden
    valleys hold."

Old Lambro and his ten young men on like a torrent
    swept,
The dust from their swift horses' hoofs like a thick
    cloud upthrown.
And Lenoula at her window stood all pensive and
    alone,
And she followed with her mournful gaze that dash-
    ing troop, and wept.

What seeth the maid 'mong those eleven riders who
    depart ?
Alas! her father goes to seek a husband for her hand—
And she sees the youth she loveth well among that
    little band :
She loves him, and none other knows the burthen of
    her heart.

'That heart hath scarce put forth its blooms ere from
    grief it fades away,
Weep, poor Lenoula! weep, for thee a life-long woe
    doth stay!

The Dance and the Grave.[1]

—Spyridon Lambros.

He sees the foaming of the lashing wave,
    He hears the roaring of the tempest wild,
He looks intent on Death, and on the grave,
    But heedeth not, for Daring is Love's child.

He heedeth not.   His light and fragile boat
    Trembles within the fierce waves' heavy swell,
Now high, now low borne struggling, yet afloat
    It touches first the clouds, then nears to Hell.

He heedeth not.   If Death is lurking there,
    Where howls the storm, or in the upheaved wave,
Or if a watery bed they straight prepare ;
    To him what is this death, and what the grave !

He heedeth not.   It is for one loved face
    Strain forth his tear-impassioned eyes alone ;

[1] This poem was written in extreme youth, Mr. Lambros having for many years devoted himself to philosophical studies alone.

One look alone to catch, one sign to trace,
  While the strong current draws his doomed skiff on.

Beyond the gulf he sees the crystal doors
  Where the high roof is filled with flashing light,
Where for the rhythmic dance gay music pours,
  And thinks of forms in joyous movement bright.

And sometimes to these doors there draweth near
  (Which the hot breath of dancers hath made dim)
A well-curled head, in angel' outline clear,
  Some straying lock to rearrange and trim—

Whilst he unhappy with the whirlpool's rage
  Sharp wrestling, heedeth not its uncontrol ;
Enough that *her* he sees, who doth engage
  His every thought, the loved one of his soul.

Well born was she, and on her snowy breast
  Flashed diamonds, and the girl was wondrous fair ;
And to her grace wealth gave its splendid zest.
  But worthless all—no woman's heart was there.

And he, poor youth, had somewhile beauty, ere
  Th' unwearied sun had marred his marble brow.
Nor gold hath he, nor gleaming diamonds fair,
  But deeper riches doth his true heart know.

Ah! what the charm of flowing silk attire,
   The flow of graceful wit, the well-turned phrase—
Could these in me divinest Love inspire
   Where they the heart's best sympathies erase ?

Long did the boatman gaze upon that door
   (Who from afar a closèd book can read),
He without hope—his boat, no rudder more,
   Nearer those frightful rocks to ruin speed.

Long, long intent he gazed; the whirlpool now
   Engulfs both boat and man, and all is o'er.
A broad sea flows, a deep deep grave below.
   Tears for the dead the running waves' outpour.

There, where in careless joy the gay feet move,
   Within is heard the poor boat's echoing crash ;
And from the opening door—a head above
   Looks on that sea the wild storm' winds that
      lash.

A sudden lightning which the darkness rent
   Showed scatter'd fragments which the wild waves
      strew ;
Not one small tear with pitying looks was blent
   Where the closed doors a smiling face withdrew.

Again the dance! again the music's swell!
  Again the glass is dim! Out, out, alas!
A man is drowning! Sad Fate rings his knell—
  Whilst others laugh, and jest, and sing, and pass.

Before the Panagia.

—Achilles Paraschos.

Within thy quiet church I come again,
   O Virgin Mother, all my griefs to tell—
I come to speak to thee of my heart's pain ;
   None other have I, as thou knowest well.
Joy of the world, thy pity on me lie ;
My Mary she is ill, I fear lest she may die.

O Queen of Heaven ! Earth's fair shelt'ring stay—
   Thy gilded picture sees me here alone.
Alas ! *she* cometh not with me to-day
   To light thy candles—dimly art thou shown.
Who will bring incense, Lady, floating high,
If my dear love, if my dear Mary die ?

I have not sought the healers, Lady mild ;
   To thee I come to make my Mary well.
Oh, by the first glance of thy Holy Child,
   By His first smile, His pure youth's thoughtful spell.
By His hard cross, and crown of thorns, I cry
To thee to save my Mary, lest she die.

Do me this good, sweet Lady, and I'll light
   A lamp above thy holy picture—fair
As her dear form, and as her pure soul white,
   Bright as her eyes to sparkle 'fore thee there.
Ah, grant me but this grace, O Lady High,
I would not that my Mary—*she* should die!

Yes, if I've ever brought thee fragrant flowers,
   If I have ever incense to thee thrown,
If I have wept thy Holy Son's sad hours
   (My Mary's name too, is it not thine own?)
Give me, oh give Life's dewy plant, that I
May give my Mary, lest that she may die.

The Child and the River.

—George Viziénos.

In silvery ripples a stream flows on,
   A child looks in it and laughs with glee.
What harm have its crystal waters done?
   What harm can the wavelets bring to me?

Two lilies, they float on the limpid way,
   And here, and there, they are crossed awhile,
So the child doth think they have words to say,
   And to him they are making some sign the
      while.

Now here, now there, he to them doth lean;
   The river it passeth along with joy;
But what do the yellow lilies mean?
   And what do they wish to tell the boy?

To a willow-branch he clingeth now,
   That little one who doth long to hear,
Alas! when suddenly snaps the bough—
   He is whirled away in the waters clear.

At once there is quench'd his eyes' sweet light,
   At once his cheeks show the roses' loss;
When down drop those yellow lilies bright,
   And lie on his body and form a cross.

What child to a river who draweth near,
   Seeth not good in all things there?
What harm can come from the wavelets clear—
   The rippling wavelets that look so fair!

The Dove. (Τὸ Τρυγόνι.)

—GEORGE VIZIÉNOS.

THE little birds in pairs
    Fly through the woods abreast ;
The little birds in pairs
    Sleep by the shrouded nest.

One only, whose poor heart
    Is wrung with grief, doth stay—
Alone all through the night,
    Alone all through the day.

Yet this too was belovèd,
    And joyed in its dear mate,
And sang for very gladness
    Of its most happy state.

But when one early morn
    They fondled as they flew,
The sportsman came, and straight
    The dear companion slew.

K

No other it desires
  To gladden and to sing ;
It seeks no other friend,
  None other love can bring.

And aye it mourns, alone
  The woods it flieth round,
And dimmeth as it drinketh
  The water-brooks there found.

From anguish and from grief
  It slowly pines away.
And there, alone, in silence,
  The poor dove died, they say.

The Anemone.

—George Viziênos.

A ROCK upon the hill-side
    Doth with himself commune ;
A streamlet runs before him
    With ever-sounding tune.

An anemone who blossoms
    Upon the barren stone,
Bends down to learn what meaning
    Lies in that song's gay tone.

And overmuch inclineth
    From the base whereon it clings ;
" What song is that which ever
    The running voyager sings ? "

A beauteous arm he singeth,
    Extending with delight,
Of a lovely shore somewhither,
    Which waits him day and night.

K *

" Would I were she," she crieth,
  " Who meets his fond embrace ! "
And the flower lower stoopeth
  To kiss the streamlet's face.

But as she down is bending,
  The river's ardour strong,
Strips from her all her leaflets,
  And with him whirls along.

Now standeth she despoilèd,
  A lone and barren stock ;
Why, why then did she loosen
  Her hold upon the rock ?

POEMS OF SENTIMENT AND FEELING.

The Poet.

—George Zalakostas.

Grief knows not sleep. Upon the mountains' height
    White mists are hanging still,
    Whilst over rock and hill
    The dawn is quiv'ring bright.

Both herbs and grass drink in the dews of Night,
    The birds with warbling meet,
    And rising breezes sweet
    On the stream cut furrows light.

Nereids unseen their golden crownlets plait
    Upon the mountain-brow,
    I' this mystic hour now
    All round the angels wait

Fair dawn, wherein all Nature breathes forth sweets
    From flower, bough, and leaf.
    The heart that feels no grief
    With joy thy radiance meets.

A poet-youth draws near a limpid spring
    With eyes suffused in tears ;
    The list'ning silence hears,
    What sighs his bosom wring !

" O joyless Night ! thy face seems like mine own !
    Yet with what witching spell
    Thy charm upon me fell
    When flowers my path had strown.

Among the trees the little birds renew
    Their songs of faithful love,
    Whilst I in this lone grove
    A fleeing shade pursue.

Yet once these woods were Paradise to me—
    Here, where soft dews are nursed ;
    Ah fool ! who Fate accursed,
    On earth would pleasures see.

Hereafter if some other come to mourn,
    And in sad tones and low
    Shall 'plain a hidden woe,
    Tell him of me forlorn—

Tell him of Chryse, full of youth and grace,
    A queen the dance among,

To whom the maiden throng
Would aye yield chiefest place:

How fine her softly pencilled brows, how sweet
Her calm eyes' gentle light!
Those coral lips so bright
In none—none other meet!

What did her youth or loveliness avail
With stern remorseless Fate?
Death looked on her but late,
Soul hunter grim and pale!

Call me not ingrate—lilies, birds, and streams!
All ye who knew her well!
Without her, can I dwell
In this vain world of dreams?

Here where I wander heavy, dull, and pale,
I would my soul could pass,
Since Life is Hell, alas!
And Death, a Festival."

Death hears, and ere the almond trees of Spring
Put on their fragrant bloom,
To his lov'd Chryse's tomb
The hapless youth they bring.

'Two trees they plant upon the sacred place :
          These cast soft shadows 'round,
          And when loud winds resound,
          Their boughs with love embrace.

To a Star.

—John Karasutsas.

O thou who in yon ether's boundless vast
   Dost show so doubting and uncertain light,
As glittering shells from depths of ocean cast,
   Now lost to view, now back, with gleaming bright :

Should that amass of diamonds which gem
   The heav'ns be God's mantle over all,
Thou art a little brilliant on the hem
   Of those thick folds which round the Maker fall ;

But if no garment, but an altar high,
   Where thousand thousand lights in worship burn,
Thou a small lamp, a spark from the northern sky,
   One holy ray wilt yet unceasing turn.

Yet if this firmament, if this great dome,
   With all its emerald and sapphire host,
Nor altar is, nor raiment, but outcome
   Of worlds on worlds in long extension lost—

Parent of Beauty art thou then—and Light!
   A sun with planets moving in thy train,
While every planet hath attendants bright,
   Like birds their mother following o'er the plain :

Then, like a giant upon shoulders broad,
   Thou bearest earths, and seas, and hills, and vales;
Myriads of towns, where strifes have long abode.
   Tell now one page of thy historic tales.

Is it with thee, O world, as it is here?
   Are thousands born, do thousands daily die?
Do thousands laugh, while thousands shed the tear?
   Are funeral, bridal lamps still passing by?

What laws doth Justice to thy children lend?
   Doth a pure freedom in thy councils speak?
Or before tyrants do thy people bend
   The knee, and do the strong oppress the weak?

O Star! whilst now to thee my eye upstrains,
   Maybe with thee are fleets in war array,
The crash of battles echoing o'er thy plains,
   And armies falling on the blood-stained way!

And yet thy children with their noise and strife
   Within one little point are closed and held,
With all thy silent dead passed out of life
   In that one glittering speck by us beheld—

That spark which glints in highest heav'n! yet this
   Nor place nor hour changeth, but holds good,
Though if Night came, and 'twere not, who would
      miss   .
   A grain i' the sands, a leaf from out the wood!

O Star! who setting, rising evermore,
   We 'mong the hosts of other stars neglect,
That faithfully thy path still goest o'er,
   Yet what thou art by us so little reckt:

When Night ariseth, thou like timid maid
   Com'st forth, the last of all the stars in space;
Scarce twinkling, when behind the hills in shade
   Thou hastest first 'mong all to hide thy face.

Unnamed the Argive left thee.   From afar—
   Now—beautiful thou comest as of yore,
Through the blue ether flashing; yet, O Star,
   A Night will come when *thou* shalt shine no more.

Last Words.[1]

—JOHN KARASUTSAS.

ERE in the grave my radiant star
    Had set in grief—when death was nigh—
Before this world she left afar,
    She breathed these words with tear-dimm'd
        eye :

O sweet Ionia's glowing morn,
    On thy gold rays my spirit bear ;
Scenes, where all earthly joys were born.
    Ye made for me, a heaven fair !

Kleinias, be consoled, I die—
    But, love, I will not leave thee—aye—
A faithful shade still following nigh,
    Living, or dead, with thee I stay.

When in some evening hushed and still
    Thou wand'rest forth in pensive mood,
And hear'st a nightingale with thrill
    Of passion sing from out the wood—

---

[1] The two first stanzas of the original of this poem are here con-
densed into one.

Then pause awhile, and ling'ring stay,
  For know that in its plaintive song
The bird but telleth in its way
  Of all that knit our love so strong.

When on thy elbow soft inclined
  Thou gazest on the ocean's swell,
And thy sad eye with brooding mind
  O'er all its purple breadth doth dwell—

From depths those purple waters lave,
  I, like a dream will quick ascend,
And in the murmuring of the wave
  Sweet whisp'rings unto thee will send.

If Winter doth the Tmôlon[1] beat,
  Or wild typhoons may slumbering lie ;
Fair Spring to thee will yet repeat
  The roses, and the swallows' cry.

When thou art happy, I'll rejoice ;
  If mournful strains awake thy lyre,
Unseen, the Muse' pathetic voice
  In poetry will I inspire.

If, when in lower darkness found,
  Pale Hades holdeth me enchained,

[1] Τομωλίτς = Μπούζδάγ.

And from above, by Kerberus bound,
　With guards and massive bolts restrained—

My tears shall even Hades move,
　And Kerberus its pity share,
As I lament my constant love,
　And my Kleinias' name declare—

Thy name—Kleinias! evermore,
　Because, dear friend, it hath been said,
In hate, or loving, faithful more
　Than all the living are the dead.

The Last May Song.[1]

—Elias Tantalidês.

Thou art come back again to outpour
    From thy wallet thy bright gifts anew;
And dost ask, O sweet May, as of yore,
    That my song shall thy praises renew.

A defaulter, in silence, three years
    I have fled from the Muses and thee;
Yet receive, although coming with tears,
    This my strain as a welcome from me.

---

[1] In this poem the poet bewails his blindness, which calamity befel him suddenly at the early age of 27. Notwithstanding this drawback, Elias Tantalidês bravely persevered in his avocation as a Professor of Literature until the end of his life, dying in 1876 when still in his prime. Notwithstanding his blindness, with the exception of this May song, his poems are especially distinguished for gaiety and brightness. Born in Constantinople, and (if we do not reckon those years in which he held a professorship at Smyrna) mostly living there, all political or national subjects were excluded from his Muse. He wrote, therefore, chiefly bacchanalian and love lyrics, which exhibit much playful humour.

L *

O how chang'd from the scenes as of old !
    O how iron the strength of old Time !
Thou dost see me, and oft have I told
    How we met in my youth's flow'ry prime.

I was first 'mong thy lovers, sweet May,
    Whilst in darkness lay shrouded the dawn,
Who in haste ere the opening of day
    From thy leaves brush'd the first dews of morn.

I was first with my song to awake
    Ev'ry echo from wood and from grove,
Ere the birds with their carols could make
    The air ring with a chorus of love.

How I laugh'd, how I leapt in my glee !
    As I bough from bough parted away ;
Like the butterflies, light-winged and free,
    So I gathered thy rosebuds, O May !

But my wings, whilst I flew, they were shorn
    By the shears of divinely sent Fate—
Not for Death, welcome now as the morn,
    But for weary life, lingering late.

So thy festival cometh not now
    As the herald of love and delight ;
All hath ceased of past ecstasies' flow
    In a life which is buried in night.

For thy May blossoms now blooming fair—
 They are *black* with the shadows of night;
And thy laugh doth not ring through the air
 In a dawning whose sun sheds no light.

And in me thou canst now nought behold
 Of the youth who once woke at thy smile,
In this body whose veins do but hold
 Just a breath of pale life for awhile.

I am furrowed with care, and my feet,
 As they stumble through pathways of gloom,
With a staff which my hands stretch to meet,
 Are but groping their way to the tomb.

We are wholly divorced, O dear May!
 Yet in grace take the off'ring I bring,
As though weeping and sighing, to-day
 I to thee this my last greeting sing.

For as now *thou* wilt come back again:
 Aye from others *we* reap; but for thee
Thou dost bring life and youth in thy train
 To transform them all, gladsome and free.

Now to thee, from the young and the strong,
 There is rising a chorus of praise;
As from me, 'stead of hymning and song,
 They are tears which are drenching my lays.

Yet take ye, O friends—take these tears,
On thy gardens of flowers them outpour,
And forgive these my lips whence appears
A complaint where a psalm should adore.

To a River.

—Achilles Paraschos.

O RIVER, flowing onwards, river dear!
   Which still with thousand voices biddeth me,
That I, unhappy, in thy waters clear
   Shall plunge; and yet it is not given *thee*
To know wherefore and whitherwards thou'rt going,
Though forward, ever forward, thou art flowing.

But I will tell thee—I—most gracious stream,
   What Fate intended for thy crystal wave,
With all the sparkles of its silvery gleam—
   In an *abyss* to fall and find a grave.
Yes, woful one, thou may'st not, canst not stay,
One common law perforce must thou obey;
O river, gentle river, thou as I must pass away.

Yet, ere thou passest onwards, look awhile,
   If thou hast eyes, upon yon lovely sky,
That gazes on thee with a tender smile,
   Nor all unheeding ever, glide thou by

The flowers that thou waterest as thou flowest,
Or the gay Earth—to darkness though thou goest.

Pause then, and haste not; look up to those skies,
   That heaven which lies mirror'd in thy breast;
See on its purple depths light clouds arise,
   Like to thy stream with snowy foamings drest.
Thou too hast dewy clouds like lilies white,
But thine are Earth clouds, they the clouds of Heav'n
    bright.

O tell me, river, hadst thou mother dear;
   What clouds begot, and bore thee, and then fled?
Ah! thou art like to man, too like me here!
   But weary am I by the years on led.
So now I seek, O river, 'neath thy wave
My heart's hot flame to quench, my burning breast
    to lave.

Thus saying, in the flowing river sprung
   A tearful bard with weighty load of grief;
Unloved by one he fondly loved and sung,
   And all forgotten where he sought relief.
The wave the youth bore onwards, nor did stay,
But onwards to the *abyss*—the wave too went its
    way.

𝕿𝖍𝖊 𝕯𝖔𝖛𝖊𝖘. An Allegory.

From Η ΧΙΟΣ ΔΟΥΛΗ—Theodore Orphanidés.

Within a flowery verdant mead
   There dwelt two tender faithful doves—
   Who knew alone of happy loves,
Of sighs or tears nor meaning heed.

The hopes that strew the path of life
   With purest joys, on them shone bright—
   And ere each morn arose in light,
The woods with their gay songs were rife.

But Winter came, and in its train
   A raging tempest, which uptore
   The trees, and spoiled what green earth bore—
And all the blossoms of the plain.

Then one—from other whirled away,
   Woke on a strange and friendless shore,
   Which the grave's silent aspect wore.
And one—amid the storm did stay.

L *

Borne by the whirlwind through the night—
  A hungry eagle—drifting on,
  Seizes this lonely trembling one
With a loud shriek of shrill delight.

But after many mourning years,
  With feet that flee the foreign strand—
  The true dove seeks its fatherland,
And back its first love' ardour bears.

But seeks in vain the woven nest
  Laid waste by many a typhoon's strife—
  In vain that darling of her life
The eagle from their home did wrest.

With loud complaints she crieth aye,
  "O God! in tears of grief I drown :
  Didst Thou not make me too Thine own,
Or merely for a tyrant's prey ?"

The Maker heard, and thus decreed :
  " Be thou, forthwith an eagle, dove,
  And swiftly on thy foeman prove
That which thou deem'st his rightful meed."

Then the frail bird ascended high
  On eagle's outstretched golden wings,
    And through the cloudlands hasting—brings
The fear that dwells with power nigh.

Quick her swift flight to slay the foe,
Upon which deed no foulness lies;
'T was Honour bade—and in her eyes
Vengeance and Love together glow.

The fate of Chios is the subject of the above poem. Chios, cele-brated as the richest and most populous of the Greek islands, whose inhabitants were gentle as well as industrious, whose women were celebrated for beauty, with a climate most genial, and abounding in fruits, became at once a desert. In the words of Trikoupis : "Thus did the so famous Chios, the island of delights, wealth, and a large population, become a place of desolation and tears" (Τοιου-τρόπως ἡ περίφημος Χίος, ἡ νῆσος τῆς τρυφῆς, τοῦ πλόυτου καὶ τῆς πολυανθρωπίας, ἔγεινε τόπος ἐρημώσεως καὶ δακρύων). Also Gordon thus describes this lovely spot : "Chios carried on a brisk trade in silk and fruit, and supplied Constantinople with oranges, lemons, and citrons. Twenty-two villages were also devoted to the pro-duction of gum mastic for the imperial harem (the Eastern ladies chewing it). The character of the Chians partook of the softness of their climate—mild, gay, lively, acute, industrious, and pro-verbially timid, they succeeded alike in commerce and literature—ardent promoters of education and passionately fond of their native land" (vol. i. p. 350). "Forty-six flourishing villages, a fine city, many splendid convents reduced to ashes, 25,000 Chians massacred, and 45,000 dragged into slavery" (vol. i. p. 360).

The Flower-Seller.

—A. Rhangabês.

Comely damsels! hither stay,
Here are flowers fresh as day:
    Shall I sell you this, or this?
Soft, softly, now, for mind—
Whiche'er the hand I find
    In my basket, I shall kiss.

What loveliness is here
In this jasmine white and clear!
    'T is Innocence!   Who'll buy?
You ask, " Is aught to pay ? "
Nay, for love I give 't away;
    Still no—ah! tell me why.

A rose! 't is love's first streak
In a blush upon the cheek,
    And kisses two 'twill cost:
It will o'er this maid prevail,
Who tender rosebuds pale
    Herself resembleth most.

Carnations ! these, they say,
Will fervent passion aye
    Within some heart inspire.
Who'll bid ? That one alone
Is *fifty ;* for this one
    Kisses *hundred* I require.

1 have here a bramble bloom ;
They say 'tis Pleasure's groom,
    And bringeth joyous gain.
Take care ! It hath a thorn,
It is but a wilding born,
    And leaves behind it pain.

With snowy blossoms sweet,
Which zephyrs love to meet,
    See, orange blossoms fair !
What mutual grace doth shine
When the bride doth them entwine
    Around her golden hair !

You know it ! Fie ! no haste,
Nor, maidens, rend or waste,
    For I have many more—
Some for the young and small,
For the grand, ay, some for all,
    From a never-ending store.

Here's honeysuckle free ;
'Tis Truth, and you may see
        That Truth all, all do sell.
How so ; none seek it ! Nay,
I'll give 't.   They turn away,
            Saying, laughing, "*Thank you well.*"

The Girl and the Leaf.

—STAMATOS VALVÉS.

It chanced one evening in May,
   The whole creation seemed most fain
Due homage to that Lord to pay
   By whom glad Nature bloom'd again.

     On the moon's bright
     And silver light
   Stood gazing a maiden fair,
     When a leaflet shorn,
     On the wind's plumes borne,
  Fell flutt'ring on her there.

" Ah ! but of perfumes this is chief,"
   Crieth the girl. " These scents which rise
Do make the fond heart drunk O leaf !
   With the odour divine of Paradise.

Who was thy mother tell to me—
   Was she the Hyacinth or Rose ?
Either my thoughts could give to thee,
   But thou dost other form disclose."

            " A stray leaf mere
            From the high hills near,
        Come I, O damsel fair ;
            But yesterday
            'Mong blossoms gay
        I was left by the roaming air.

    And of their fragrance caught a part
        Whilst dwelling 'mong those neighbours sweet
    As in thy pure and spotless heart
        Behold ! thy parents' virtues meet."

Night and Day.

"Am I not now beyond all measure blest?"
  Cried the fair Night unto the bright-faced Day;
" I—with the light of myriad stars am drest,
      And moon's soft ray—

But thou—my sister—lo—thou art most poor!
  Thy form is bathed by one star's gleam alone,
Which—if the wing of a small cloud pass o'er,
      Is dimmèd soon.

Nor canst thou boast sweet Aphrodite's light—
  Nor cluster of the blooming Pleiades,
Nor mighty Jupiter—that planet bright—
      Thou hast not these."

" Yea verily—thou justly—well hast said,"
  The pure Day answered all aglow her sky:
" But with thy many gems which radiance shed
      Shin'st thou as I ?

Dear Night—the Beautiful doth not appear
  In borrow'd lustres from a host—arrayed,
Which when the one true Brilliancy draws near—
  Will pale and fade."

Would'st thou the lamp of glory?   Darkness flee—
  'Thy crown be roses of the Daybreak born;
E'en thou—blind owl! friend of the sun must be,
  And hail the morn.

Life.

—George Viziênos.

One and all with thought profound,
Strive how they may compass round
    To learn what power and design
    Spirit to matter doth assign.

I, a youth of temper gay—
Wilt thou listen while I say
    Why and how the *all* is done
    Thou dost fret thyself upon?

God of pliant matter weaves
A cage, which openings five receives,
    And those windows seen within
    Are the senses placed therein.

Then amid that cage so fair
He a bird doth 'close, who there
    In its own tongue talketh now
    Of all that it observes below.

M *

Whilst the cage doth strong remain,
There the bird still findeth vain
    All attempts away to fly,
    And Life with Health goes merrily!

But when the cage begins to spoil,
Then the bird will strive and moil,
    Till it openeth some way
    Through the which to flee away.

And to former nest returned,
All that it hath seen and learned
    'Twill some day in converse clear
    Tell to birds of other sphere.

But should Nature ever find
A cage without the bird confined;
    She will lift it, and will bear
    To her home with kindly care—

And with zeal will work and strain
To give it warmth and life again,
    For it seemeth chilled and cold:
    Worn it is, alas! and old.

LEGENDARY POEMS.

The Last Dryad.

—John Karasutsas.

A THOUSAND winters have despoiled my lustrous
    verdant hair,
But when spring smiles, and fresh leaves to the bare
    boughs bring repair,
        I bloom again.

So far agone yet seem to me my first years until now,
That if some other, or the same old self I dare not
    know—
        If I remain.

What sweet sound that! was it some old companion's
    voice that spoke?
No; the north wind hath fiercely blown, and 'twas
    my own lov'd oak
        That whispered low:

Ah, sad one! thou forgettest too that thou hast lived
    beyond
The law of Fate. With thine old age the breezes
    make no bond,
        But scorn thee now.

                                   *

Man's race once flourished here: in years past hither
　　came
The hunters, and the rustics brought their toils to
　　snare the game
　　　　These woods among.

When the wild beast went slowly forth from out his
　　thicket lair,
The Sun God, as those hunters, was not so swift, so
　　fair,
　　　　So brave, or strong.

With booty safe, when came the dexterous youth,
　　he little knew
What other secret wounds had made those arrows
　　which he threw,
　　　　Unknowing where.

The nymph who, breathless and unseen, for him had
　　waited long,
Found all her kinship with the gods, 'gainst love to
　　make her strong,
　　　　Unavailing there.

When to my shade he wearied came, with what fond
　　zeal and care
For his refreshing, out from my dark leaves I shook
　　the air,
　　　　Bade the zephyrs haste.

For he to me was much more dear, yea, dearer far
    than they—
Those dusky Satyrs who once came, my ears pollut-
    ing aye
        With lyres unchaste.

The Marriage of Earth.

—George Viziênos.

From height to height, from height to height,
  Old cuckoo calls again,
Bidding the birds for a wedding bright
  To raise the nuptial strain.

And the wingèd guests rejoicing all,
  To the country quick repair—
To joy in the gladsome festival,
  To joy with the wedded pair.

Each tree puts on its festal gown,
  And musky-scented flower;
The herbs with dewy diamonds strown,
  As well befits the hour.

And Nature opes her temple door,
  The wide and pathless wood;
And calleth to her sacred floor
  All life for worship good.

The sun comes forth with cheerful brow,
  And hastes the lamps to light;
For dews are flashing on each bough
  With sparks from emeralds bright.

The rose into the censer flings
  Her frankincense most sweet;
Each bird within the choir sings
  The holy anthem meet.[1]

And God's own holy hand doth wreathe
  The crowns upon each brow,
For wedded is the widow Earth
  Unto the young Spring now.

[1] See notes on Greek marriage service.

The Rain.

THE daughters of the Ocean,
  Their water. vases filled,
Go rising up like cloudlets
  To the heav'ns calm and stilled,

To find some flower to water,
  Or rose-tree blooming fair,
That they may call forth blossoms,
  To place amid their hair.

As here and there they're gliding
  With timid hearts of fear,
The children of the high hills,
  The boist'rous winds draw near;

And boylike, they, those maidens,
  With their filled urns, pursue,
And chase them as though lev'rets,
  And they had game in view.

With one of charms surpassing,
  Whose hair flows loose and long,
They seek to sport some moments,
  And join in dance and song.

So here and there pursuing
  This timid maiden throng,
Their waving garments seizing
  They hold with grasping strong.

Now here, now there yet striving,
  Till with a sudden blow
They break the urns of water,
  And the water forth doth flow.

And thence below it rusheth
  To every field and plain ;
And this is why it raineth—
  Through this we have the rain.

The Trees.

ALL the dear shady trees
   Are children the earth hath borne ;
The hands they lift to the breeze
   Are the boughs their forms adorn.

They lift them in prayerful strain,
   And sorrow awhile they pray
That Heaven, who holds the rain,
   Doth see them athirst each day.

And beholding them, high Heav'n
   Remembers the olden days,
When the Earth for his bride was given,
   And the wedding was joy and praise.

So down from his throne he bends,
   And calleth a willing cloud,
Whom forth to the hills he sends,
   To the woods and forests proud.

" To those trees athirsting go,
   To the woods which droop and sink,
On the dear ones let water flow,
   Give them that they may drink."

And the cloud goes forth with will
   From the firmament above,
And she raineth upon the hill,
   And rains on the woods with love.

And the earth has a secret joy,
   That she is remembered still,
As flowers without alloy,
   And fruits her fair bosom fill.

So out from her gladness sweet,
   And joy which doth much abound,
Abundance, and harvests meet,
   She giveth the country 'round.

For he who would prosper, lo !
   He must plant trees fair and good,
And leave them to freely grow
   Till they make the thick shadowy wood.

'That we too may have the rain,
    And the beautiful fields of green,
And in barren Hellas again
    Be plenty and verdure seen.

Evening.

THE bright impatient Sun
    Glides down unto the West;
A cloud hangs forth a veil
    To shroud his glowing breast.

For clad all o'er with gold,
    And most exceeding fair,
With open arms the Evening
    Is waiting for him there.

And with the healing streams[1]
    She doth refresh him now,
And bringeth cooling dews
    To bathe his heated brow.

Now fasting and aweary
    He sitteth at her board,[2]

[1] An allusion to the popular superstition of *healing waters*, which are supposed to cure every malady of mind or body.

[2] 'Ο ἥλιος παέι 'σ τὸ γιῶμα—meaning literally *the sun is going to dinner*, idiomatically for *the sun is setting*—is a popular expression.

Where—breathing savours sweet,
  She setteth forth her hoard.

Whilst these he scarcely tastes,
  His head falls on her breast,
As he turns to his belovèd
  Within her arms to rest.

And she—who so long time
  Hath waited for him there—
Now stretcheth out her hands
  And strokes his golden hair.

Then going up on high
  With lit lamps in their hands
There come from out the West
  The timid starry bands—

And each of these draws near
  To look behind the hill
Where the nymph in tender tones
  Her love is pleading still.

The Storm.

Th' unthinking clouds in squadrons
  Come riding from the North,
And on the hills descending
  Their heavy charge give forth ;

From ev'ry peak around them
  Thick wreaths of vapour pour—
With lightning' flash, and thunder
  Begins the battle's roar.

Instead of spear and bullet—
  Hailstones and rains they wield—
Which on the Earth descending
  Despoil the seeded field.

Instead of sword—the rustic
  Doth grasp the spade and hoe,
Nor can arrest the battle
  That floods the lands with woe.

N *

So—looking up to Heaven—
  To God he lifts his eyes,
Whence dimming tears are falling—
  " Help ! help Thou me !" he cries.

And God—who hath compassion
  On the man's good heart and fear ;
To bring him help and comfort
  Doth bid the Sun appear.

As on either side the heavens
  The sun and clouds are seen,
The fair and graceful rainbow
  Comes stepping in between.

" Foes ! sheathe forthwith your weapons—
  And bid your thunders cease,
Of old was I made in heaven
  The treaty and bond of peace—

Which the Maker wrote in colours,
  In colours which still remain,
That the husbandman beholding
  May see what is written plain.

For the red is the crimson wine,
  The yellow the golden wheat,

And the green is that which giveth
  Th' abundant olives sweet.

So that he may send forth ever
  His liturgy of praise,
And with ardour light the tapers
  Of ever-living rays."

The Seasons.

THE widow'd Earth is loved of suitors four,—
    Four faithful wooers true ;
Each after other cometh with his store,
    And spreads before her view
      All he doth bring as dow'r.

The Spring than all the others is more gay—
    A youth with feelings sweet ;
For love alone through all the livelong day
    Her ev'ry wish to meet
      He gladly hastes each hour.

He summons all the birds, and bids them sing
    Her praise in cheerful choir,
Each scented flow'r and rose bedew'd doth bring ;
    All things that joy inspire
      He wills shall her surround.

With zeal and ardour clothing her all o'er
    In many radiant dyes,

Whilst his full hands exulting much, outpour
    The perfumes rich which rise
      Her garment all around.

The Earth looks on him : gladness fills her brow,
    His wooing well hath sped.
She saith impassioned, " Spring ! I love thee now ;"
    And yet she doth not wed—
      Oh wherefore—wherefore—why ?

The bolder Summer cometh with ripe brain—
    A full-grown man and strong.
Her threshold as he crosseth with his train,
    The Lady stays not long
      To cast her first love by.

Her flow'rs in due time into fruitage grow :
    The blade brings forth the ear ;
With flashing sickle quick doth Summer mow
    All grains that ripe appear,
      And harvesteth right well.

He bringeth her abundant wheat and rye,
    Her children dear to feed ;
And her broad garner-house he pileth high
    With thousand varied seed,
      Earth's treasury to swell.

N *

The Earth looks on him, gladness fills her brow,
    His wooing well hath sped :
" Summer ! " she cries, " I love *thee* dearly now ; "
    But yet she doth not wed—
      Oh wherefore—wherefore—why ?

Sick Autumn with his wan face draweth nigh,
    Whom one glance doth delight ;
Whilst on her threshold, with fond-pitying eye,
    The Lady changing quite,
      All former love throws by.

Crimsoned her lovely breast, whereon he strows
    Fruits, and the clust'ring vine :
Sir Autumn plucks the ripe grapes as he goes,
    While kisses intertwine,[1]
      And casteth them in press.

The trodden wine is drunk, the must inhaled,
    Which swelling song inspires
With hopes that youth has o'er the years prevailed,
    And boyhood's ardent fires
      Have come old age to bless.

The Earth looks on him, gladness fills her brow,
    His wooing well hath sped :

---

[1] $\mu\epsilon$ $\phi\iota\lambda\acute{\eta}\mu\alpha\tau\alpha$. The poet by this means that whilst gathering the grapes, the young men behind the vines often snatch a kiss from the maidens.

She cries, " Sir Autumn ! yes ! I love *thee* now ; "
    But yet she doth not wed —
      Oh wherefore—wherefore—why ?

The tyrant lord, Old Winter, with white hair,
    Doth harm her in his love ;
As he her threshold passes—straightway there
    The Lady yet doth prove
      All old loves quite cast by.

In secret he makes tremulous her breath,
    And chilleth her warm blood ;
Within her veins creeps soulless life—like Death,
    And sadly doth she brood
      In cold mistrust and fear.

Sir Winter all in raiment white is drest,
    With beard like driven snow ;
He bringeth pure white garments o'er her breast
    As a nuptial robe to throw,
      For his bride in church to appear.

The Earth looks on him with a scornful brow,
    Ill hath his wooing sped.
She cries, " What, wintry Sir, I love *thee*—No ! "
    And so she doth not wed —
      Ah wherefore—wherefore—why ?

The handsome Spring to her will come again,
      Her own belovèd boy ;
And whilst the birds ring forth in glad refrain,
      She'll wake again to joy
      As her first love draws nigh.

March.

MARCH brings the broidered gown that April wears ;
The mountain streams within his arms he bears,
      And makes the plains grow bright
      With radiant gleaming light.

The trees within their bark yet shivering stay,
The blossoms in their buds yet dream away.
      Nor has the Mother Earth
      To her flowers given birth.

" Trees, 'tis March calls.　Away your idlesse fling ;
Flow'rs ! ope your eyes, and from your couches spring
      To greet the magic hand
      Which decks the joyous land.

For I am that glad month who ev'ry year
Kiss the young flow'rs and haste their colours here,
      And for each maiden fair
      A faithful youth prepare."

The flow'rs awakening hear, and sweet lips ope,
The trees half raise their eyes in verdant hope,
    And rending buds show clear
    That roses too are near.

The Almond tree an artful nymph doth seem,
Who roused from sleep and called from out a dream,
    Her naked charms embow'rs
    With nuptial robe of flow'rs.

" Hail to the comely youth in vision bright,
Who in my dreams did wed me yesternight;
    What fair gifts doth he bring
    Before my feet to fling? "

Coverlet and couch from the snowy North he bears,
The night is joyous, but when dawning nears,
    The Rime with chilling arms
    Doth grasp those glowing charms.

Her bridal dress i' the morn a shroud appears
The grieving Earth doth melt in misty tears,
    But Noon with golden ray
    Tears the cold veil away.

Metamorphoses.

A MOTHER had born to her children four,
      Four children had she borne ;
She nourish'd them, rear'd them, made each a dow'r
      With a heart as bright as morn.

And she sought, and did wed them to, folk of estate,[1]—
      And rich in all household gear ;
And they homesteads kept—and were deemed right great
      Athrough all the country near.

But—for the ageing mother—Fate
      Had evil gifts in store ;
Her goodman died—and in sorrowing state—
      A widow was she—and poor.

When it came to pass she fell sick one day—
      The time was sad—and drear,

---

[1] Νοικοκυραῖοι = *aristocrats*, who were merchants holding their own
ships in the islands of Hydra and Spetzai.   See note, p. 263.

So a stranger she called—and bade him—away—
      To bring all her children near.

" To my dear son go—bid him hither speed—
      For I am sick with care."
He went;—but the son must his vineyard weed,
      Nor hath he time to spare.

She said, " On his body let bristles grow
      For aye—for evermore."
Straightway to the hills did the bad son go—
      In the hedge-hog's form he wore.

" To my daughter go—and bid her here—
      For I am sick with care."
He went;—she was spinning silk fine and clear,
      Nor had *she* time to spare.

" Let her spin—her thread shall lengthen still,
      But woven cloth ne'er be."
And th' unpitying child with a spider's skill
      Vain cobwebs aye spun she.

" To my second daughter go—and say
      That I am sick with care."
He went;—but she said she must wash her array,
      Nor time had *she* to spare.

"Let a trough be her raiment henceforth," said she,
    "And unwashed, unchanged keep."
So the pitiless child must a tortoise be
    On the earth to crawl and creep.

"To my third daughter go, and bid her here,
    For I am sick with care."
He went; but before his return she was near;
    Had she then time to spare?

"Why on thy hands doth dough appear?
    Why on thy fingers flour?"
"I was leav'ning when the news came, mother dear,
    But I came the selfsame hour."

"Let thy flour be pollen, thy trough a hive;
    And since thou time hast found,
May all thou touchest whilst thou shalt live
    With honey sweet abound."

Thus saying, she smiled as she went to sleep,
    For aye, for evermore;
And thence her daughter the form doth keep
    Of a bee with honied store.

So forth she flieth on joyful wings,
    By flower and bloom carest,

> And to every creature a blessing brings—
> She—whom her mother blest.

The bee is popularly called the blessing ('Ευλογία) of God among the peasants in many parts of Greece, which are familiar with the above legend, in consequence of the mother's blessing her dutiful daughter. The value of the bee for the sake of its honey to large numbers of country people can hardly be over-estimated.

The Building of St. Sophia.[1]

In the great city day and night
The King doth study how to build
The Church of Saint Sophia fair.
From every part he doth invite
All men in works of science skilled,
Who plans and drawings must prepare.

The Architect designs doth bring,
The Secretary spreads them out,
And layeth them before the throne.
The King looks on them sorrowing,
Upon his face sits anxious doubt,
Unworthy deemeth he each one.

" God is," saith he, " all power and light.
Alone that beauty which doth shine
Reflected everywhere around.

[1] This is a popular legend in Thrace, where bees are held in great estimation.

His church should therefore show His might,
  Perfection glow in every line,
    And Heaven's semblance there be found."

Then all the builders sadly kneel,
  And all the great ones of the court
    In silence their due homage pay.
For each and every one doth feel,
  Not *his* the craft for what is sought,
    And none can word in counsel say.

All through the night with thoughtful brow,
  Each strives to fashion in his mind
    The plan which doth before him lie.
None heeds the coming Sunday now,
  But toileth on, for none can find
    The heart to join in worship high.

Yet when the morning dawneth there,
  They see the sacred tapers pass;
    They hear an old voice tremulous sing.
It is the Patriarch who doth bear,
  Straight going from the church and mass,
    The blessed bread [1] unto the King,

---

[1] The *Antidoron* (ἀντίδωρον) is the bread which has been offered
for the service of the altar, but which has not been required for
consecration. This blessed bread is broken into portions, which
towards the close of the liturgy are distributed to the worshippers
by the clergyman who stands for the purpose outside the holy doors.

Who, bending from his throne doth kiss
　　Those aged hands which to him bring
　　　The blessing and the Holy One.
Yet some way happeth it amiss,
　　For the bread falleth from the King
　　　The thick-furred lion skins upon.

The King his sceptre casts below,
　　And leaves at once his royal seat,
　　　To search with care around and near.
It must not on the earth lie low,
　　Lest it be trodden 'neath the feet,
　　　And some one fall in judgment drear.

Whilst thus the King with troubled face
　　Before his throne bends low his head,
　　　Where still he hopes that gift may lie;
A bee he seeth near the place,
　　Which holds in its small jaws the bread,
　　　And from the window forth doth fly.

Often a portion is carried home from church to some member of a
family who may have been debarred by sickness or some other cause
from attending divine service. It is always reverentially eaten,
and valued as a token of church fellowship; and as it dates from
very early times, it is possible that it may be traceable to the
love-feast of the Primitive Church. In the old French rituals it
is found under the name of *pain béni*.

Straightway a crier he decrees
  Shall to the market-place be sent,
    And thus declare the royal mind.
" A purse of gold !   Who keepeth bees
  Let him now search with close intent,
    That he my blessèd bread may find."

Then all men seek with close intent;
  Yet from their seeking nothing gain
    Other than wax or honey sweet.
The Master-Builder's thoughts are bent
  On seeking, and with eyes full fain
    A marvel doth his vision meet.

Within a basket woven fine,
  Wherein a hive is moulded fair,
    Glitters and gleameth somewhat bright;
No yellow wax thus e'er can shine,
  No honey sweet he seeth there,
    But sculptured church with carvings light.

Its domes are like the heavens above,
  The columns like thick woods uprise;
    The floor may with wide Earth compare.
Never will Christian song of love
  For God's great praise and worship rise
    Within another church so fair.

He, then abashed before the throne,
  Prostration maketh low and deep,
    And open'th out the temple's plan :
" We all are sinners—every one—
  Nor one among us who doth know,
    Or God's magnificence can scan.

Thy blessèd bread to cherish, lo !
  With what amassing treasures filled,
    See this good bee hath hither brought—
The Highest aye to honour. So,
  Let the Great King a temple build
    Like to this church so fairly wrought."

The King to God doth low incline—
  " Beauty and Power unto Thee
    Ever," he cries, " be grateful praise ! "
Three times he kisses the design,
  And then declares the firm decree,
    " Thus shall ye Saint Sophia raise."

LOVE LYRICS.

The Parting.

—Aristomenês Provilegios.

When with recalling love I told
   My country's climate fair,
How a green carpet was unrolled,
   How roses in the wintry air
   Bloomed with the tints of Spring ;

How that the sun's ne'er dimmèd ray,
   Piercing the ether blue,
Was lost within that ocean way,
   Which ever lengthening to the view
   One purple breadth would bring.

" Ah ! " sighed she sadly, " each fond word
   That floweth from thy mouth,
Shows thee by home's deep longings stirred ;
   But thou, true child of thy dear South,
   Remember *me* when there."

" In the blue colour of her skies,"
  I said, in grief's despite,
" Again I'll see thy gentle eyes,
  And in our Phœbus' golden light
  Behold thy shining hair."

Two Sonnets.

Ah! now at last I freely breathe to-day.
  The pain, and all the gnawing and unrest,
  Which so long wrestling with did weight my breast,
Is over.   Conquered Love hath flown away.

O blissful calm! I hail thee with thy train
  Of many angels 'round thee fair and bright;
  My spirit walks forgetful, to the light
Of the blue ether rising once again.

Now heal'd—as if so pitiful a wound
It ne'er had known, my heart doth daily bound,
And seeks—its past commotions to renew.

As when the sailor—saved, though tempest tost,
Through the fierce wintry winds so nearly lost—
Longs his drear wanderings to commence anew.

THE harpsichord thy fingers lightly press,
　　While thy rich voice with sympathetic tone
　　Opens to me the gates of realms unknown,
And lights untrodden paths of happiness.

Thy song doth cease, when floweth o'er my soul
　　The strength divinest of the wordless strain,
　　And then, as though with mimic speech, again
Music brings back in pictured form the whole.

When long I to fall prostrate at thy feet,
And all the fairest gifts that e'er can meet
In heavenly places in thy lap to pour.

For both the power of thy Music's spell
And thy sweet feeling face their impress tell,
Deep in my spirit all things else before.

The Osier Bough.

—GEORGE DROSINÊS.   From Εἰδύλλια.

" IF thou pluck'st me not as thou go'st by,
Thy love it shall fade away and die."

So sings the dewy osier
Early in the morning,
Holding to the traveller
Her flower-boughs in warning.

An old man if it chanceth,
The name of love then hearing—
On the other side he passeth
And turns his head with fearing.

But if a black-eyed maiden
And her lover hither stray—

A bough of the dewy osier
They haste to cut straightway.

For they are troubled in heart, and fear
Lest e'er unto them that curse come near.

Snows.

From Εἰδύλλια.

The sun shines, filled with glowing light,
Our earth is mantled o'er with snow ;
In Nature only, to my sight
A pair like *heat* and *cold* doth show :

Yes, in a blue-eyed little maid
I see the very same exprest,
Within her eyes the fire displayed,
Yet bearing snows upon her breast.

A star which shines on high,
(The earth is chill and cold)
Doth glitter and doth flash upon
The snows which her enfold.

A tender breast which loves
In hopeless grief and woe,

Is like the star which casts
Its light upon the snow.

———

WHAT are the soft white snows,
    That are falling from the sky,
Which the driving north wind strows,
    On the mountains piling high?

Is it cotton in heaven grown,
    Which the tender flowers outfling?
Or is it the finest down,
    Plucked from an angel's wing?

A Diamond.

From Ἱστῷ Ἀράχνης.

It once so happed a crystal fragment lay
Unmarkèd long upon some thistles sere,
When on a sudden kissed by the sun's ray,
Its brilliant sparkling all behold, and say,
" Ha, what a lovely diamond is here!"

My love it is, that clotheth her with light!
For all she is a maiden no more fair
Than others, but for me—a star of night,
A flower, an angel, or a bird o' the air!
For you 'tis glass, for me a diamond bright.

Pity 'Tis.

From Ἱστὸι Ἀράχνης.

THEY talk as though in April 'twere alone
That roses blossom and that lilies flower;
But now we're in old January's power,
Yet on her cheeks and on her red lips shown
Lilies and roses opened full I see——

But pity 'tis they do not bloom for me.

Why, Mary?

From Ἱστὶ Ἀράχνης.

WHEN I tell thee on thy mouth, so small and sweet,
The hues, the scent, the dews of roses meet,
  Thou tak'st it well and smil'st, Mary;
But when I would (a little dew to sip)
A bee become, and fly to thy red lip,
  It angers thee; but why, Mary?

P

FOLK SONGS.

The Only Daughter.[1]

—George Drosinês.

"Tell me, O lovely maiden, whence do thy graces
    flow,
How did thy mother nourish thee, what care did she
    bestow :
With sugar did she feed thee, that thou art aye so
    sweet ;
Was milk thy drink, for thou like milk with white-
    ness art replete ;
Did she bathe thee in rose waters, for thou bloomest
    like the rose ;
Made she a bed of downy plumes whereon thou
    might'st repose,
With sweet musk for a pillow, that thou of musk
    may'st smell ?
" My good and darling mother, my mother deeming
    well,

[1] Mr. Drosinês, in his Folk Songs, has caught all the spirit and piquancy of those songs which he heard from the lips of the girls of Euboea, several of which he gives us in 'Αγρότικαι 'Επίστολαι. They are, however, not *reproductions*, although possessed with the same feeling.

With sugar hath not fed me, white milk for drink
    nor gave,
Nor that I might be more than fair, did with rose
    water lave ;
She gave me no musk pillow, no bed of down to press ;
But my kind mother nourish'd me with many a fond
    caress ;
And with her loving kisses she all this sweetness
    sent,
And with her tender blessing this balmy perfume
    lent.
Thus was I reared on love alone, and bloom in beauty
    drest,
For I am an only daughter, a maiden much carest."

The Maiden and the Sailor.

A MAIDEN, by her window broidering,
Looks out upon the broad and purple sea ;
And still she sews and sews, soft murmuring,
And still she sews and sews, and thus sings she :
O silly madcap South Wind, gently blow,
And thou, O North, some little prudence show,
For I have my beloved one on the sea ;
And I await the joyful Easter-tide
When I shall wear the flow'r crown of a bride,
And he in bridegroom's scented garb shall be.[1]

The North Wind heard, and pitying breathed a sigh ;
But the offended South waxed grim and wroth !
" The silly South, my damsel, ne'er am I,
But the dreadful South, when I go angry forth ;
For bosoms numberless have I made dark,
Made mothers widows, orphaned babes beside :
I overwhelm the sailor with his bark,
And I will make thee widow ere a bride."

[1] See note of sailor's wedding at Spetzai.

With syphoon then she roused the sleeping sea,
The waves like swarthy demons whirled around ;
His shapely boat was overborne, and he,
The hapless sailor youth, the lover, drown'd.

The maiden wept not when the tale they told,
Nor spoke one word, no sigh her bosom tore.
She fix'd her eyes where yet the ocean roll'd,
And 'gan to broider deftly as before.
And as she sewed and sewed,[1] thus still sang she :
"O silly madcap South Wind, gently blow!
And thou, O North, some little prudence show,
For I have my beloved one on the sea."

The travellers who journey by her door—
They hear her, and they wipe the tears away.
The fishermen who sail along the shore—
They hear her, sighing as their boats they stay.
For the maiden, for the sailor, pitying pray.

---

[1] To prepare the clothes for her dowry is the chief care and em-
ployment of the peasant girl. Not only does she make all her garments, sewing and embroidering them most exquisitely, but she *spins*
the cotton and wool, of which they are composed, *dyes* and weaves
it with her own hands. Some will have as many as 40 ὑποκάμισα
alone.

The Gifts.

" SENT forth by my good master, a merchant young
    am I ;
For him I'll buy sweet sugar, honey of price I'll
    buy.
O damsel sweet of speech who hath met me on the
    way,
Wilt thou thy honey-sugar'd lips sell me for gold
    to-day ? "

" My lips I do not sell, but I'll give them with the
    rest,
With all my other dowry, to the youth whom I love
    best."

" A gardener am I, damsel, of lilies I have store ;
But thy face hath fairer lilies than aught I've grown
    before.

               *

Then stay, thou lily-cheeked one, and to me two lilies
    sell,
In my garden I will plant them, and rejoice in their
    sweet smell."

" 'The lilies of my face I keep to give them with the
    rest,
With all my other dowry, to the youth whom I love
    best."

" I deal in silk, O fair one ! one moment prithee
    stay,
And tell me for how much thou'lt sell thy plaited
    hair to-day ;
It falleth o'er thy shoulders in trim and even row,
In golden sheen and glistering, as finest silk threads
    show."

" Nor yet my shining yellow locks, for they go with
    the rest,
With all my other dowry, to the youth whom I love
    best."

" I am a wealthy goldsmith, and have jewels that I
    prize,
But, girl ! for how much wilt thou sell thy blue
    and gentle eyes ?

They are a pair so full of light, so like to sapphires
    true,
That I will make of them two rings, with stones of
    heavenly blue ! ”

“ My eyes, in sooth, I may not sell : I give them
    with the rest,
With all my other dowry, to the youth whom I love
    best.”

“ Dear maid, I am no goldsmith, nor gardener I’ll
    prove ;
I am the poor youth thou wilt take, the youth whom
    thou dost love,
Who all night long keeps watch and ward before thy
    cottage door,
And to his little tambourine thy beauties singeth
    o’er.”

“ If thou’rt the youth I love so well, then I have
    nought to say,
For what to others I sell not, to thee I give away.”

The Witchcrafts of Love.

High on the brow of the mountain, from the busy
    world away,
There sitteth a cunning woman—a woman weird and
    gray.
A maiden goeth in early dawn, and with pleasant
    words doth greet,
She layeth eggs in her mantle, and wheat ears at her
    feet.
" How chanceth it, fair damsel, this uphill path
    thou'st won,
To come and see the wizard dame who sitteth here
    alone ? "
" To tell thee all my anguish, to confess to thee, wise
    dame,
Unknowing both my mother and my brother, here I
    came
Because I love Kostantios, and he careth not for
    me ;
Alas ! he loves another, and 'tis she his bride who'll
    be."

" If Kostantô he love thee not, what can my skill
    avail ?"
" Oh, charm thou *once*, and then straightway his love
    for her shall fail ;
Oh, charm thou *twice*, and then forthwith will love
    for me prevail."

" Why, maiden, ask'st thou charms from me ? what
    could my art devise ?
For thou hast charms more potent far in your two
    bright black eyes ;
And in thy mouth so small and sweet, your hands so
    white and fair ;
For they do all the youth bewitch, and e'en old men
    ensnare.
Go back unto thy village, girl, and make thee all
    good speed,
And when the next glad festal day comes round, then
    take thou heed,
Put on thy white embroidered gown,[1] thy finest
    softest vest,[2]

---

[1] ὑποκάμισον, the under and chief garment, composed of thick and fine white cotton, close to the throat, and down to the feet, with wide sleeves, and all richly embroidered.

[2] σιγγοῦνι, a sleeveless long vest of white woollen, reaching beyond the hips, and open at the chest ; also embroidered round the bottom.

Thy skirt of red with silken flow'rs,[1] thy chains across
    thy breast,[2]
And bind a yellow kerchief then thy graceful head
    around.
Then let your place amid the dance near Kostantô be
    found,
And be not shamefast overmuch, but raise your head
    awhile,
And press his hand whilst up to him you lift your
    eyes and smile.
Let none then call me wizard dame, nor my renown
    spread wide,
If Kostantô doth seek thee not to ask thee for his
    bride."

The dawning breaketh sweetly which St. George's
    Day [3] doth bring,
When on the threshing-floor the youths and maidens
    dance and sing.
The pretty damsel dances then to Kostantaki near

---

[1] ποδιά, a short skirt of crimson cloth, often most exquisitely
worked in silk, with the most harmonious blending of colours.

[2] γιουρντάνι, numerous connected chains of silver, to which are
appended a multitude of silver coins of different kinds.

[3] St. George's Day, old style, would be the 6th of May, when
the harvest in many parts of Greece would be over and thresh-
ing began. The wheat-ears show ripe in the beginning of
April.

With all her silver ornaments,[1] and all her broidered
    gear,
And by degrees less shamefast, she doth lift to him
    her eyes,
And Kostantô then trembles, and his heart throbs
    with surprise ;
But when the maiden smiles on him, and presses
    soft his hand,
Kostantaki feeleth faint and sick—he loseth all
    command,
And he forsakes the dance straightway, and to his
    home doth glide.
But ere the hill is darkened, ere the sun sinks o'er its
    side,
Proposals fair for her he sends, and asks her for his
    bride.

[1] ἅρματα. All the silver ornaments, chains, bracelets, brooches,
clasps, &c., are classed together as ἅρματα = *weapons*. Mr. Drosinês,
in his Ἀγρότικαι ἐπίστολαι, in speaking of this appellation, remarks
that he supposes the name has been given because "through them
men's hearts are wounded."

The Old Klepht.

The lads are eating and drinking, gaily their songs
arise.

A captain of Klephts, an old Souliote, beholds them,
and listening, sighs.

"Come hither, old man, wilt not thou now sing us a
better lay?

Come, give us a song of the olden time, of the days
long past away."

"What can I tell you, giddy boys, how can 1
laugh and sing?

My voice is husky with many years—my heart is a
changèd thing

Since I was a gallant Pallikar—a lusty youth and
strong,

None then could face me in the dance, excel me in
the song.

I clomb the hills and mountains high, as with the
Turks I warred;

I went down 'mong the villages—the girls by love
    were snared—
The mothers who beheld me, they all wished me for
    their son—
The damsels who looked on me strove how I might
    soon be won—
Some two or three fell sick indeed and pined away
    and died—
And others donned the serge and left the world and
    all beside !
But I no woman gladdened and a wife I ne'er have
    wed—
For I was a Klepht at Agrapha, and sore it had
    bested
If I had ta'en a wife with me up to our Klephtic
    hold !
What pleasures—and what joys for her could there
    her life enfold ?
Could I leave her in the village—and bemoan for her
    on high ?
No—as a widow I have lived—and widowed I shall
    die.
'Tis well for you lads, well, Rouméli's sparrow hawks
    so gay—
For you have now your freedom—lead a merry life
    to-day—
Your parents are not slaughter'd, and your houses
    are not spoil'd—

Q *

Nor in the Turks' hareems are your sisters dear
    defiled.
You do not scour the mountains nor in rocky fast-
    ness hide—
But through the villages you walk safe by your
    mother's side—
And come and take your place i' the dance that you
    may charm my eyes
With your tall and dapper bodies, and your waists
    of slender size—
And bid me to recount to you—my youth and the
    olden day
When as it is with you—'twas then, my April and
    fair May.
But now old January's snows have compassed me
    around
From hour to hour—I sit—and wait—till Charon
    hath me found."

The Slave.

THE Turks came down and burnt the homesteads
    near,
The Christian folk dispersing, fled for fear ;
The children from their mothers' arms were torn,
The sisters from their brothers far were borne,
Parted—a wedded pair of two days old.

The lovely bride to slavery was sold
In the city, whom a tyrant vizir bought ;
The husband as a Klepht the mountains sought.

Twelve years passed over since that hapless day.
She saw the Aprils who bring in the rose,
She saw the Januarys come with snows ;
And she with grieving beat her heart away,
As a partridge which a narrow cage doth close.

Then some good Christian, pitying her pain,
For seven thousands [1] her redeemed again ;

[1] 7000 γρὀσσα = piastres.

And sent her to her own dear country back.
But many woes had agèd her, alack!
And many tears had marred her visage fair,
And many bitter thoughts had blanched her hair.

Not one in her own country knew her—none.
" Hail!" cried she, " men and lasses, every one—
Know ye not here Gerometros' son's son,
Whether he lives—hath gone away—or died?"
" He liveth, and is chief here far and wide,
A fair wife had he, lost when yet a bride;
But he hath ta'en another still more fair,
And hath two sons to lighten every care."

As a taper wasteth [1] so her visage failed,
White as the cotton plant her poor lips paled;
Returning on the road she trod before,
She prayed the Abbess at the convent door—

" Give me the gown of black! the cloth of hair!
A Turk's foul kisses brought my youth despair;
For twelve long years no church my feet have trod."
All through the night then prayèd she to God.
She kissed the cross and pictures, wept and sighed,
But with the dawn for very grief she died.

---

[1] The simile of " tapers wasting " is a very favourite one, and any
one who has seen the rapidity with which they are consumed at
the Greek festivals, melting away in a few seconds comparatively,
must admit the expression as used to be felicitous.

As they her body in the earth would lay,
Kostantios Gerometros came that way ;
He claimed her for his own, and stood beside,
Kissed her, and knew she was his first dear bride.

The Hercids.

It was a gay young cavalier, a comely youth enow,
Who rode forth from his home unto a village far away
To keep Elias' festival whereto he'd made a vow.
He started with the dawn, the sun now told the close
    of day,[1]
When the youth drew up and paused beside a flowing
    river's brink,
That he and his aweary steed might rest awhile and
    drink.
But soon as he dismounted and had loosed his bridle
    rein,
There came the sound of women washing garments
    in the flow.
He tied his horse unto a bough and turned him round
    again,
To see if they were cousins fair or damsels he might
    know ;

[1] πάει 'σ τò γιώμα.   See note to " Evening."

But none are of his country, nor the soft singouni [1]
    wear ;
Their robes are all of purest white, and white their
    mantles fair,
And o'er their shoulders floating fall full three arms'
    length [2] of hair.

Their every look was lovely, their lips with smiles
    were sweet,
Their eyes were black as gown of priest, straight
    brows, long lashes meet.
The comely youth then knew at once that these were
    Nereids fair, [3]
As sisters, all alike in face and form and graces rare ;
And one among—than all the rest was yet more
    charming shown,
Who wore upon her stately head a shining golden
    crown.,

The youth drew near and greeted them with greetings
    deep and low—

---

[1] Singouni. See note to "The Witchcrafts of Love."

[2] The measure in Greece is by the $\pi\hat{\eta}\chi\upsilon s$ or arm's length, being
two feet.

[3] A belief that there are Nereids still lurks among the peasantry
in remote districts, especially among the women. Only last summer
(1884) an embroideress who was disposing of her embroideries in
Athens, was asked why they were always more or less stained.
"Κυρία," she exclaimed, in answer to my friend's inquiry, "*it is the
Nereids who do it when they borrow them for their baptisms.*"

" All hail, O Queen! Companions hail!" "Hail
        youth with comely brow."
" Fair ladies, who your garments sweet wash in the
        crystal stream,
Will you not wash for me my cloak with dust and
        heat defiled ?"
" With joy, with joy, O rustic brave whom gallant
        youth we deem."
And once, yea twice, the queen's fair hands washed
        well the mantle soiled.

The youth then dons the mantle, and he hasteth to
        the feast,
And wheresoe'er he standeth and wheresoe'er he goes,
One to the other whispereth, and asketh of the rest,
" Whence came that sweet and musky smell that all
        around arose :
Is it a bough of the wild vine, or incense wafted near,
Or is it a perfum'd damsel bathed in musk who cometh
        here ?"

" 'Tis not a branch of the wild vine, nor holy incense'
        breath,
It is not a damsel who hath bathed in musk that
        scents the air ;
It is alone my mantle from the crystal runlet 'neath,
Which the Lady of the Nereids washed with dainty
        hands so fair :

It hath scented me, and my good steed, the roads
    that branched aside—
The travellers—and all the church—the country far
    and wide—
But not with me befitteth it such mantle should
    · abide :

Come hither then, fair maidens, and range you in a
    row [1]—
All who, in dance excelling—who chief in singing
    prove—
And she who danceth best of all—whose song doth
    sweetest flow—
To her my mantle I will give—and she shall be my
    love." [2]

[1] For account of festival dancing and dance songs see Appendix
Notes, p. 284.

[2] Antoniadès in his Κρῆτηΐς, whilst introducing the "Nereids,"
gives a very good solution of the origin of these wild fancies among
mountaineers, the inhabitants of lonely hills in all countries being
more given to flights of fancy, and superstitions than the children
of the plains. He pictures the solitary shepherd—with his flock,
his dog, and his pipe—arriving in the shades of evening at a stream
surrounded by rocks. All kinds of misty wraiths might soon be
conjured up as he rested there, or played his simple music, while
the darkness closed around him. The usual result, however, of inter-
views with the Nereids is not of the nature of the above meeting of
the youth with the lady "Καλῶ." On the contrary it is generally
described to be signally fatal, for if the shepherd or traveller be not
allured by the charms of one in particular into unhallowed love,
the mere beholding them is of itself sufficient to bring on a disease
which baffles the skill of the most skilful physicians, and can only
be removed by the exorcisms of a cunning woman.

NOTES.

NOTES.

ALI PASHA AND HIS MOTHER HAMKOS.

"The renowned barbarian Ali Pasha, the celebrated vizier of Epirus, was born about the year 1745, at Tepeleni, a small village on the banks of the Aoüss or Voïoussa, near the spot where it' issues from the gorges of Klissura. His family, whose name was Issas, or Jesus, an appellation still common in the East, came originally from Asia Minor with the hordes of Bajazet Ilderim ;[1] and his grandfather Mouctar was one of those who fell at the siege of Corfu, by Diannun Cozia in 1716. He left three sons, of whom the youngest, Veli, after exercising for some years the profession of a bandit in the mountains of Albania, returned to Tepeleni, murdered his elder brothers, seized upon the property of the family, and became the first Aga of his native village. He subsequently married the daughter of the Bey of Conitza, Khamcos, or Hamcos [2] as it is now written, by whom he had two children. Ali, the future lord of Juannina, and his sister Chaïnitza, after a

---

[1] Sir James Emerson Tennent's *History of Modern Greece*, vol. ii. p. 381. According to Pouqueville they were Albanians by descent ; the story of their Asiatic origin is that of Ali himself.

[2] More generally called "Hamko."

life of crime and debauchery, died while his offspring were still in their infancy."

On the death of Veli, the widow Hamko, upon the plea of defending the rights of her son and daughter, Ali and Chaïnitza, against the sons of a former union, headed the bands and tribes herself, and led them forth against the neighbouring peoples. In one of these marches she fell into an ambuscade, and was taken by her enemies with her two children and thrown into the prison of Gardiki. She was afterwards ransomed, the money being supplied by a Greek ; but some insults received from the Gardikiotes remained rankling, and young Ali was educated to become her avenger. Step by step he rose to riches and power, solely, as he said, by following the maxims of his mother,[1] wherefore to her throughout life he was thoroughly devoted. More than forty years after the insults from the Gardikiotes, Hamko, dying of a painful disease, sent for Ali to receive her last commands. He did not reach her until she had expired, but his sister repeated to him the infamous bequest, and hand-in-hand before the dead body of Hamko, Ali and Chaïnitza swore to exterminate utterly Gardiki, men, women, and children, and to lay it waste. "*Showers of tears accompanied his oaths.*"

It was not until fifteen years after this that an opportunity presented itself for carrying out his mother's will (written as well as verbal) regarding Gardiki. His sister, had he been so minded, would not, however, let him forget their joint bond, and in 1812 the time came. As cunning as he was cruel, he hoodwinked the French consul by

---

[1] See conversation of Ali with Mons. Pouqueville, Consul of France at Janina for fourteen years, in *Histoire de la Régénération de la Grèce*, tom i. chap. x.

declaring [1] to him that he would make Gardiki, which he was just on the point of acquiring, "la fleur de l'Albanie," whilst he had just received a despatch from his sister, saying that the women must be at her disposal, "Je ne veux plus coucher que sur les matelas remplis de leurs cheveux." The Gardikiotes were a mixed people, Mahometans as well as Christians, and the order for the massacre was indignantly rejected by Omer Brionês (Vrioni), who refused to shed the blood of Mahometans. The next order was given to a battalion of Mirdites. Their leader, Andrè Gozzolino, whereupon exclaimed, "We kill men without any defence! put arms in their hands and we will go against them as warriors." Athanasius Bagias (Thanasy Vayia or Vaiia) then *offered* himself, and to him was the destruction of Gardiki deputed, and the details of this dreadful event literally fulfilled the commands of the mother and the wishes of the daughter.

"THE FLIGHT."

" The Flight" celebrates the great success obtained by the Souliotes under Lambros Tsavellas [2] over Ali Pasha on the 20th July 1792. The Vizir had left Janina with 15,000 men, who had all sworn upon the Koran to exterminate the Christians of Souli. The Souliotes were celebrating their festival of flowers when they heard of

[1] *Histoire de la Régénération de la Grèce*, par Mons. Hugues Pouqueville, tom. ii. chap. iv.

[2] Written Tsavellas, Tzavellas, and Zabellas. In this and other names I have followed the Greek and English authors quoted, although they differ.

the approach of the Turks. Abandoning their villages
and plains they gathered together, and awaited their
enemies in the defiles of the mountains. Their women,
headed by Moscho, the wife of Tsavellas, and their
daughter Caïdos, hurled down stones from the heights,
and broke the column of the assailants, and in this
position the advanced body of the Turks was engaged
and entirely beaten without any quarter being given,
and only the rear-guard escaped, leaving seven hundred
and forty dead. This defeat caused a panic among the
Turks, and Ali fled precipitately by night to Janina.—
See Pouqueville's *Histoire de la Régénération*, liv. i.
chap. vi.

KATZANTONÊS.

In 1806, impelled by the cruelties exercised in Cephalonia, Ithaca, and Leucadia, a general rising took place
in Corfu, encouraged by Russia. Thither went Cadgi
Anton (Katzantonês), "couvert d'armes brillantes,"[1] with
his five brothers, the Botzarês', and other captains, who
took oaths of fidelity to Russia, Katzantonês swearing
never to lay down his arms until Greece was free, and
placed under the sovereignty of the Orthodox ruler.
The triple alliance of Turkey, England, and Russia against
France, altered the views of the Greek patriots, but Katzantonês remained faithful to his first idea. This wild
mountain hero or Klepht, renowned as he had been for
his many exploits, miscalculated the strength against

---

[1] Pouqueville.

which he had to contend, and the numbers which could be brought against his small force. Ali Pasha had kept constant watch upon this valiant chief, who was celebrated no less for beauty of person [1] than for his prowess. The Albanian, Veli Ghekas, who was in the service of Ali, was sent against him with a regiment of Albanians. After some reverses, and when wasted by a slow fever, he, in company with his brother, George Hasotês, sought the heights of Agrapha, thinking to recover health and strength in its mountain air. He remained some days in a monastery there, but not feeling assured against espial, he, whilst still weak and ill, left, and with his brother took refuge in a cave. A monk or priest who brought them food betrayed them. Sixty Albanians surrounded the cave, through whom George Hasotês, carrying his sick brother, endeavoured to cut his way. They were, however, both made prisoners, and taken to Janina, where they were beaten to death by hammers. Katzantônês, being enfeebled by disease, is described in some accounts as having given way to cries, and as having been reproved for this by his brother, but the popular version is that he died exultant.—Pouqueville, &c.

A popular (folk) song makes him victorious. It represents Katzantônês as inviting Veli to Agrapha to show him how Klephts fight—" Νὰ 'δῆς τὰ κλέφτικα σπαθιά, τὰ κλέφτικα ντουφέκια," and after a combat of three hours, " τρεῖς ὥραις μὲ τὴν ὥρα," Katzantônês and his eighty-three comrades kill Veli and his pashas—

> "'Ο Κατζαντώνης 'στ' Ἄγραφα μ' ὀγδόντα τρεῖς νομάτους,
> Τὸν Β—Γκέκα 'σκότωσε, καὶ τρεῖς μπουλούκ πασάδες."
> —'Ανθολογία Μικαλοπόυλου.

---

[1] He is described as of middle height, with eyes of fire, long black moustache and shady (νεφελώδεις) eyebrows, agile in limb, with a sweet voice.

THANASY VAYIA (Θανασης Βάγιας).

THE name of Thanasês (Athanasius) Vayias (which I have thought is better rendered by phonetically anglicising it as Thanásy Vayia [1]) is perhaps held in more unqualified detestation by the Greek people, especially by the inhabitants of Epirus and Thessaly, than even that of his notorious master, Ali, on account of his being himself a Greek. After the horrible massacre of Gardiki he was advanced to the post of Ali's secretary; but upon the downfall and death of the Pasha, although he escaped with his life, he fell into the extreme depths of poverty, hated and shunned by all men, or, in the words of a contemporary to whom Valaôritês appealed for information concerning him, "ἐψόφισε, φίλε μου σὰν σκύλος" (he was starved, my friend, like a dog); and when he died, his body with difficulty obtained burial. His widow, bare-foot and in rags, wandered from door to door imploring alms, until she also died, said the same authority, "Κύριος οἶδε ποῦ" (God knows where), adding, "Εἶναι δίκαιας ἡ κρίσαις τοῦ μεγάλου Θεοῦ"!—*Introduction to "Θανάσης Βάγιας," by Valaôritês*—"Μνημόσυνα," Athens, 1868.

> "*Reach me but the light*
> *Which you each evening kindle*" (p. 48).

In the humblest dwelling there is generally a small lamp or taper—lighted as often as possibly can be afforded—before a picture of the Blessed Virgin or favourite saint. I have seen some—usually a common coloured print—so begrimed with smoke and faded by years that it was not possible to discover a trace of any feature therein.

"A fleshly form hast still?" ("Πές μου δὲν ἐλυωσες") literally = "Tell me, art thou not dissolved?" There is a belief

---

[1] The French and Italian "Vaiia" is, I think, the truest equivalent for sound, as the name is popularly pronounced.

among the Greeks that the bodies of the wicked after death are delayed returning to their elements, their souls being still confined and retained in them. The souls of those who have been excommunicated or cursed not being released from their bodies, are thus the phantoms which appear to men. "After death may thy body not be dissolved" is the closing form of excommunication in an MS. in the church of St. Sophia of Thessalonica. Mons. Pouqueville states that he read the following therein: "He who has received any curse, or has not fulfilled the pious commissions left him by his parents, his body remains entire."

" *When oil and earth, &c.,*" Ὅταν σου ῥίξανε λάδι.

When the deceased has been anointed with *prayer oil* (analogous to the Roman extreme unction), the lamp or glass into which the oil and wine were poured, with what may remain in it, is thrown into the grave; also the ashes from the incense then used. This custom of anointing is seldom now followed, but many statements have been made by different writers relative to throwing oil in the grave or over the deceased before placing the lid on the coffin (which is done at the grave).—See "Greek Burial Customs," *Folk Lore Journal,* June 1884.

KLEISOVA.

" Pursuing the same system of reducing the outposts one by one, they [the Satraps] resolved to assail the convent of the Holy Trinity, a tower seated on the shoal of Klissova, half a mile to the south-east of Messalonghi, and garrisoned by 130 Roumeliotes with four small guns, under the command of Kizzo Tzavella. On the morning of the 6th of April their rafts and gunboats opened a heavy fire against it, while the Turks and Albanians of Kutahi plunged with impetuosity into the swamp, and wading across, tore down the exterior palisade; and having no scaling ladders, and being unable to get into the tower, recoiled in disorder, when the Roumêli Valesi, riding forwards to animate his troops, was shot through the thigh with a musket bullet. Ibrahim then ordered Hussein Bey to advance at the head of two regiments of Arabs, and with culpable obstinacy persisted until sunset in exposing them to be butchered, the insurgents from the loopholes picking off at pleasure the miserable Africans who stood up to the middle in water, resigning themselves to death. At length, after Hussein Bey and many other persons of distinction were slain, the Pasha sounded a retreat, whereupon Tzavella sallied out of his tower, boarded and carried seven launches that were aground, and set up a trophy composed of 1200 muskets and bayonets. This was the bloodiest day Messalonghi had yet witnessed, upwards of 1000 dead bodies of Turks and Arabs floating about the lagoon, which was actually discoloured with gore; thirty-five Greeks fell in defending Klissova, and as many were wounded."—*Gordon,* vol. v. p. 258.

[We feel pleasure in citing two signal instances of bravery displayed by the insurgents. In the heat of the action, the Khiliarch Drosinis (accompanied by a youth of seventeen years of age, and nine soldiers), loading a canoe with water and cartridges for the garrison of the tower, shoved off in the face of the enemy's flotilla; and although four of his comrades were killed by a cannon ball, and five turned back, pushed through to the islet. Constantine Trikoupi in a passara (or pinnace) armed with a three-pounder, gallantly engaged the Egyptian gunboats until she sank, when he and his men swam to Klissova.—*Gordon.*]

THE MARRIAGE OF EARTH.

" Holy anthem meet."

THE anthem referred to consists of the following troparia, which occur in the marriage office of the Greek Church :—

"Exult, O Isaiah, for a virgin has conceived, and brought forth a son, Emmanuel, God and man; the East is His name; Him do we magnify, and call the Virgin blessed.

"Ye holy martyrs, who have fought the good fight and obtained the crown, pray unto the Lord to be merciful to our souls.

"Glory be to Thee, O Christ our God, the glory of the apostles, the joy of the martyrs, whose preaching was the Consubstantial Trinity."—DR. KING's *Rites and Ceremonies of the Greek Church*, p. 250.

While the above troparia are being sung, the bride and bridegroom, having their hands joined together and held by the priest under his epitrachelion (stole), (with the witnesses holding their crowns), walk in circular procession three times, the *circle* being held to be symbolical of the *eternity* of their union.   Until this procession takes place, the ceremony may be interrupted ; *afterwards* the union is complete, and the couple are man and wife.

SAILOR'S WEDDING AT SPETZAI.

A MARRIAGE in a sailor's house is a very important event. The invited guests begin to arrive at about noon, and as soon as a guest appears he walks straight into the parlour and takes the first empty seat.   The groom is purposely dressed in his coarsest clothes, his beard two or three days old, and his stockingless feet in an old pair of shoes. When the last guest has arrived, the important performance of "shaving the groom" begins.   A chair is placed in the middle of the room, and the barber, with boy assistant, enters with a prodigious quantity of soap, oils, and *perfumes.* . . . Then three or four of his intimate friends take him into the next room, from which he emerges in half an hour quite transformed in appearance.   He is now ready to start for the bride's house, preceded by two musicians, one playing the violin and the other the banjo, followed by all the guests.   On reaching the bride's house, the groom stops on the threshold and bows three times.   His future mother-in-law kisses him, and puts a coloured silk handkerchief round his neck, which he puts in his pocket. Each of the bride's female relatives lays one on his shoulder, which he puts into a basket. The bride is then led out, and the two processions walk in separate lines to the church, &c.

When the bride quits the parents' house, the bridegroom's party leaves a live chicken in her place.—*Among the Greek Islands*, by N. Botassi, Greek Consul in New York—*Oriental Church Magazine*, March 1879.

METAMORPHOSES.

> " *Folk of estate*
> *And rich in all household gear.*"

" μὲ νοικοκυριό " = with aristocrats. The rich owners of the merchant vessels of Spetzai and Hydra (which latter small island had from olden times always retained an aristocratic form of government) were, before the war of Liberation, the holders of ships which traded at all the ports of the Mediterranean and the Black Sea. "In this way, between the years 1800 and 1820, these islanders made large fortunes, and the money was kept in cisterns built for this purpose inside their houses. It was with these monies that they armed and equipped the vessels which so successfully contended against Turkey's three-deckers."—*Among the Greek Islands.*

MYRIOLOGIES.

" With wailing dirges weep " (p. 26).

Myriologies = Μυριολόγια, or wailings for the dead, are still practised by the peasantry in outlying districts, and occasionally by the same class in more civilised centres. They are generally relatives or neighbours who perform this service, but sometimes—when these do not offer—hired mourners. In character they resemble the Irish *caione* (pronounced *keen*) of former times, as will be evident to any one who compares the writers upon these customs as they came under their own observation. The account given by Guillétiére, who was present at the funeral of a young Albanian, coincides exactly in the feelings expressed in the improvised myriologies of the assembled relatives with that given by Ross in his " Traits of the Irish Peasantry." For myself, I can ever recall the effect when, whilst living at the foot of Mount Lycabettus in 1880, I heard a funeral wail break the stillness of early dawn. I had seen at sunset the unrepressed grief of the relatives of a woman who had just died in a little cottage opposite, at the open door of which they —the women—loudly complained and wept. No distance of time can make dim the recollection of the mournful and shrill myriology. It was but a minor cadence of four semitones, alternately rising and falling, but it was enough to express the lowest depths of sorrow.

SUPPLEMENTAL POEMS.

The Destruction of Psara.[1]

(Η ΚΑΤΑΣΤΡΟΦΗ ΤΩΝ ΨΑΡΩΝ.)

—DIONYSIUS SOLOMOS.

’Σ τῶν Ψαρῶν τὴν ὁλόμαυρη ῥάχη
Περπατῶντας ἡ Δόξα μονάχη,
Μελετᾷ τὰ λαμπρὰ παλληκάρια,
Κὰι ’ς τὴν κόμη στεφάνι φορεῖ
Γενομένο ἀπὸ λίγα χορτάρια,
’Που εἶχαν μείνει’ σ’ τὴν ἔρημη γῆ.

ALONE—on Psara's blackened height
Walks Glory—musing o'er the site
Of many valiant—daring deeds.
A crown upon her brow she wears—
Made of the scant and withered weeds
The desolate earth in silence bears.

---

[1] The destruction of Psara, and the devotedness of its inhabitants, equal, if they do not surpass, the other tragic episodes of the War of Independence. The number of captives made was comparatively small. The larger amount was killed either when—after hoisting the Greek flag, with its motto, "Death or Freedom" (’Ελευθερία ἢ θάνατος)—the magazine was voluntarily fired, or by flinging themselves into the sea. The remnant was reduced to slavery or massacred, the total being about 17,000.

Anthoula.

—Dionysius Solomos.

'Αγάπησέ με, 'Ανθοῦλά μου, γλυκειὰ χρησῆ ἐλπίδα,

ANTHOULA! darling! hope's sweet golden flow'r!
I saw and loved thee in the selfsame hour!
On the green sward thine eyes were bended low—
Bright with two little pearls—by grief decked so,
Thou wept'st thy mother—blaming her—who left
Thee in the world—an orphan—and bereft.
Ah! keep thee, dear! from wand'ring in a wild
Where maidens oft by wily words are guil'd.
Where go'st thou, simple dove—alone—wilt be
'Mong snares outspread? Anthoula—come with me!

The Orphan's Death.
(Ο ΘΑΝΑΤΟΣ ΤΗΣ ΟΡΦΑΝΗΣ.)

—Dionysius Solomos.

Πές μου, θυμᾶσαι, ἀγάπη μου, ἐκείνη τὴν παιδοῦλα
'Οποῦχε στὰ ξανθὰ μαλλιά νεοθέμιστη μυρτοῦλα;

TELL me—dost thou remember, love, that charming
    little maiden—
Whose golden hair with freshly gather'd myrtle spray
    was laden,

Whose mouth was like the virgin bloom of thirty
 petalled roses [1]—
Whose eyes were blue as are the tints which heav'n
 above discloses?
Who—ever—when the shades of even fell, would
 wander—lonely—
And ever near was following her little lambkin
 only—
Whom we upon the dreary shore beheld where she
 was singing,
In plaintive tones, of all the beauty sweet Spring-
 tide was bringing?
Alas! and as her song she sang—she looked upon
 each billow
With so much grief—as though—thou said'st—she
 saw her grave's wet pillow.
Unhappy! in the hollow road I met her as I
 tarried—
But four were they, who on their shoulders then the
 maiden carried—
And over all her corse were spread—diffusing scented
 showers—
Rose, eglantine,[2] and hyacinth, with musk and violet'
 flowers.

---

[1] τριαντάφυλλον is the popular name for rose, but is also used
to represent a distinct kind—"ῥόδον" and "τριαντάφυλλον" being,
as in this poem, coupled together. Theophrastus calls some roses
"Ἑκατοντάφυλλα."

[2] In calling the thirty-petall'd rose an "eglantine" I wish to
show that two distinct roses are meant by the poet.

Her eyes that erst shone out like stars were quenchèd
    now for ever,
With crimson ribbons tied around her hands were
    bound together.
Ay me! as down the rock they came, those four the
    maiden bearing—
None but the little lamb was found who still by her
    was faring.
But withered were the flowerets all that she for its
    adorning
Herself would pluck and wreathe afresh with dawn
    of every morning.
Alone—the lambkin followed her and called upon
    her bleating,
Ba-a—ba-a—still ba-a—as though it were a very
    child and greeting ;
The bell yet hanging at its neck as down the steep
    it bounded,
Close—close unto the narrow bier a silv'ry *tin—tin*
    sounded.
This—this—my dearest—this was she—the lovely
    little maiden—
Whose golden hair with newly gathered myrtle spray
    was laden.

Vintage Song (ΤΡΥΓΟΣ).

—ATHANASIUS CHRYSTOPOULOS.

Καθαρώταταις παρθέναις
Μὲ κισσὸν στεφανωμέναις.

COMELY maidens—hither now—
Each with ivy-wreathèd brow—
  Back your sleevelets lightly fling
  To the vintage hastening.

In the right hand's firmer clasp,
One and all the keen blade grasp,
  In the left hand for your need,
  Basket of the woven reed.

So—with joyous laugh and song,
To the vineyard dance along—
  While our lips in kisses meet,[1]
  As we pluck the clusters sweet.

Hey—for the grapes all fresh as dew!
Hey—for the grapes of purple hue!
  Luscious is the joy that blends—
  In the gifts good Bacchus sends!

[1] See note to " The Seasons," p. 196.

The Three Favours (ΑΙ ΤΡΕΙΣ ΧΑΡΕΣ).

—Athanasius Christopoulos.

> " *Μὶαν ὡραίαν ἀγαποῦσα*
> *Καὶ τὸ νεῦμά της ζητοῦσα.*"

From a maiden lov'd and fair,
  Sign I seek with tender care,
That she deem me not amiss—
  Craving—only—one small kiss.

Softly beams her smile as she
  This permission granteth me—
Kissing her sweet mouth—I'm fain
  To pray for—yet one kiss again.

This vouchsafing—down she bends,
  And a *second* favour lends,
When above my kiss I stay—
  And a *third* thereon I lay.

" A third!" crieth she, " thou'st ta'en thyself!
  Now by Aphrodite's self
'Tis insolent—and overbold,
  Not e'en ' By your leave ' out-told!"

" Light of mine, the crime efface,
  And a *fourth* give thou for grace;
Give't, and straight I'll swear to thee,
  Insolent no more I'll be."

Laughs the wilful one outright—
  And my lips doth gaily smite—
" *Three* the Graces are," doth say,
  So with *three*—beloved—stay."

The Desire (Η ΕΠΙΘΥΜΙΑ).

—Alexander R. Rhangabés.

Στὰ χρυσᾶ μαλλιὰ ἐφόρει
Κόκκινο λουλοῦδ' ἡ κόρη.

A MAIDEN in her golden hair,
A red, red, rosy bloom doth wear;—
    "O give," I cried, "O give it me,
    None other gift I'll crave from thee."

She off'reth it, all blushing o'er,
With hand as white as lily flow'r;—
    "Give me thy hand—O give it me,
    Nought else," said I, "I ask of thee."

Her soft hand glides into my own,
Awhile her eyes she casteth down;—
    "Give me that look—yea—give it me—
    No more, in troth, I'll seek from thee."

On me a glance like fire doth stay,
Yet on her mouth a smile doth play;—
    "Upon those lips—one kiss grant me—
    Then—nothing more—I ask of thee."

To me her lips straightway she leaves,
The while her snowy bosom heaves;—
    "Give me that bosom too—give me—
    Nought else—I swear—I'll seek from thee."

Then—as the bending cypress bows,
Herself within my arms she throws.—
    "Now that I have thee—hold thee—here—
    No more—nought else—I ask for—dear!"

Home Sickness (Η ΝΟΣΤΑΛΓΙΑ).

—Angelos Vlachos.

" Τὶς πνοή, φαιδροί μου ξένοι, τὴν 'ερήμην μου θυρίδα."

What breeze, bright strangers, to my window dreary
Sent you, adorning it with radiant wing?
Who sent you—joy—hope—bringing me—aweary—
Who bade you to my dwelling hie—to sing
     In gladsome choir, O birds?

Saw you not 'gainst my window it was snowing—
How my hot breath had dimmèd every pane?
Thought you to find there—boughs with blossoms
  glowing,
The murmur of whose leaves might join thy strain
     Of melody, dear birds?

Or—lest the forceful South to far lands carry,
Seek you the shelter of a friendly roof—
Selling your song—awhile in warmth to tarry—
Or came ye for a crumb—in my behoof—
     Poor hung'ring birds?

Come—let me warm you—in my young arms folding
Close to a heart that throbs 'neath icy chill;
Exiles! in me an exile sad beholding—
The joy I left—here asking vainly still,
     As ye seek warmth.

Within your eyes I'll view a bright sun beaming—
And from your bill draw breath of country dear—
I'll kiss your wings, and find upon them gleaming
A drop of dew—an Attic morning's tear.—
                        Welcome, dear birds!

Tell me, from fatherland, fair travellers, speeding—
Still shineth Phœbus in a heaven as blue?
Still is the nightingale the chorus leading?
Still chirps the cricket 'mong the grass and dew
                        Its merry lay?

Like powder'd diamonds do the stars yet glister?
Do orange trees their flow'rs on lovers pour—
Their vows who 'neath their faithful shadows whisper?
Fair is Earth's nuptial chamber as of yore?
                        Tell me, sweet birds!

Yes—yes—your joyous warbling this is telling,
Your little eyes' bright sparkle this bewray'th,
Whilst my heart's depths within—with your tones
        swelling—
Another mystic voice in joy' throbs say'th—
                        Dear birds, 'tis true!

But—tell me—do those happy ones whom sweetly
Life, like a careful nurse, doth lull to sleep—
Think yet of him—once in their midst—and meetly
Heave the deep sigh, whilst tears their eyelids steep,
                        Remembering me?

Or—lost my name behind my footprints fleeting,
Like the ship's track which bore me far away—

And home returned—for me—a stranger's greeting !
And my warm love see then—their love's decay !
          Shall this be mine ?

Silent ! alas—thy silence I'm divining—
In my friends' hearts love lives not as of yore !
On my friends' lips my name hath died out—pining—
Within their souls—remembrance lives no more—
          Forgotten all !

Let them forget !—yet, strangers, if, returning
To Attic skies, when chilly North winds drive—
Say that I asked for *them*—my soul with yearning
Wrestleth—for in their love alone, I live !
          In gladness—you !

Tell them—thro' stifling clouds I still seem viewing
My fatherland's clear sky—wide-spread and fair ;
One sunlit ray, in fancy, brings renewing—
I live in mist—but breathe the Attic air,
          O birds ! around.

Tell them—yet, birdies, 'stead of telling—thither—
On your brown pinions would you bear me on—
Travelling with you—as ye came—travellers—hither?
Ye fly—alas ! by north winds borne along—
          A prosp'rous voyage—Farewell !

Elegy on George Gennadius.

From "Tears" (ΔΑΚΡΥΑ).
—George Zalakostas.

*Τίς νὰ μοὶ δείξῃ τὴν γῆν, ἥτις κρύπτει τὸν ἄριστον
πάντων;*

Who now will show me the earth where the noblest
    of all is concealèd ?
Shadowy cypress I long to implant on the spot where
    thou'rt lying,
Longing my knee low to bend, and to sow there a tear
    and a flower.
Vainly!—alas! all in vain—for a trace of thy tomb
    I am seeking,
Vainly I seek for a token wherein is some words'
    consolation,
*Here the apostle of light and the father of learning is
    sleeping !*
Name—although none—yet enough—it would tell
    me that there thou reposest—
Though—all ill-judging, the sod hath no ken of the
    great one it shroudeth.

Close the Lyceums! Lament, O ye Muses, with
    sorrow unbounded !

If—in the days of our grief, he was borne to his grave
    with no honours—
If—by his people—his country—no marble be raised
    to him ever!
If—there be given nought else—thou—a wreath of
    the dark cypress weaving.
Write of his life, Mnemosyne, O mother revered of
    the Muses!

Whilst but a child—poor and needy—athirst yet for
    wisdom and learning,
Led by a destiny loving his feet unto Dacia which
    guided,
There was he given to drink of the milk of the muses
    by Lambros:[1]
Those were the days of our weeping—a people
    enslavèd thy burthen!
Yet didst thou cherish a twice linkèd hope in thy
    tongue and religion.
Lost had Hellas been for ever of faith and her lan-
    guage unmindful.
Glory to thee, O Gennadius! to thee, her brave son,
    be the glory!
Twenty long years, thou, still waiting, wast teaching
    the language of Plato—
When—for the fetters of slaves was exchangèd the
    sharp flashing falchion—
When—in the marvellous struggle, transformed was
    the goad to a jav'lin.

[1] Lambros Photiadès.

Then—then—at once from the school of wise Germany
    hastily fleeing—
Speddest thou straight to the land that was drenched
    with the blood of the martyrs,
Where there were wrestling in conflict two principles
    ever contending.
Here was the Truth—there the Falsehood—and ours
    was the Christ—theirs Mohammed!
What time the host of our spearmen the redoubtable
    Favier[1] was leading
(He who the flag of the cross was but hoping o'er all
    to see waving)—
Cam'st thou to Karystos[2] with him, as orator camest
    and soldier—
When the satrap—the Arabian—the country of
    Pelops was smiting,
Others as careless beholders unmoved the great
    danger were viewing—
Standing alone in the midst of the champions in
    wrathful contention,
Thou, by the power of reason—assuaging their anger,
    beheld them
Lowering straightway their weapons—and each one
    the other embracing.

Filled was the chalice at last as the counsel divine
    had decreèd!

---

[1] General Favier, who had been with Marmont in the Napoleonic
wars, and who formed the first *regular* Greek corps, and under
whom Gennadius served.

[2] Karystos, a small town in the southern extremity of Euboea.

Strong were the comrades in arms who the Porte's
    goodly host overwhelming,
Hither came bearing along of brave Maison[1] the
    valiant battalion.
Trembling—the Arab he fled—while cursing us—
    then who were freemen!
Thirty long years yet again—thou—the well doing
    high-priest of learning,
Thou—who wilt aye be remembered—the whole of
    thy race wast instructing;
Yet, for thy children, how scant is the morsel of
    bread thou art leaving!

Close ye, O desolate children, the darkening door of
    his dwelling!
Close the Lyceums! Lament, O ye Muses, with
    sorrow unbounded!
This was the last of my tears, and in this my most
    heartfelt bewailing.

[1] General Maison was the commander of the French expeditionary
corps sent to occupy the Morea, and expel the Egyptian troops at
the close of the struggle.

NOTE TO ELEGY.

GEORGE GENNADIUS, one of the most prominent figures in the Greek struggle for Independence, was born at Doliana, a small town in Southern Albania. His father, a priest of the Orthodox Church, was the head of one of the oldest Greek houses, claiming descent from the family of George Gennadius Scholarius, the first Patriarch of Constantinople after its conquest by the Turks,[1] which family had originally emigrated from the island of Scio.

After his father's death, which occurred when he was a child, Gennadius was sent to his uncle, the abbot of one of the Greek monasteries in Wallachia. The Danubian Principalities, governed at that time by Greek Hospodars, were the refuge for all Greeks who thirsted alike for liberty and learning. Those enlightened princes favoured the spread of education, and established schools, which were soon rendered famous by the teachings of Eughenios of Doukas and Lambros Photiadês. The latter great master and patriot having discerned the fervent enthusiasm of the young Epirote, and his devotion to learning, cultivated

---

[1] There is in the British Museum a small but rare volume which has upon its title page a woodcut which represents the meeting between Sultan Mohammed II. and Gennadius outside the walls of the conquered city. Gennadius was then only a simple monk, but so renowned for his erudition as well as his piety that he was called upon to explain to the Sultan the doctrines of the Christian religion. By means of this exposition Gennadius was enabled to allay the ferocity of the Sultan, and to secure for the Patriarchate those immunities and privileges through which the Greek Church kept alive the spirit of the nation under Turkish oppression. This fact has been recorded by Gennadius himself in the volume referred to, viz., "*De synceritate Christianæ fidei. Dialogus qui inscribitur* περὶ τῆς ὁδοῦ τῆς σωτηρίας ἀνθρώπων, *id est, De via salutis humanæ,*" published for the first time in Vienna, 1530, by James Alexander Brassicamus.

this love for the literature and glorious traditions of his
enslaved race ; and Gennadius soon became his favourite
pupil.　He afterwards repaired to Germany to study medi-
cine, hoping therefrom to alleviate the untold miseries of
his countrymen.　But there was in his character, as was
evinced by his after career, such an admixture of almost
feminine tenderness with the heroic nature, that, after
three lectures on anatomy in the dissecting room, he was
prostrated by sickness.　Henceforth applying himself
solely to philosophical studies, and having taken honours
at the University of Leipsic, he returned to Bucharest,
and was unanimously chosen as the successor of his great
master, Photiadês.　In those days there was no more
honourable position to which the ambition of a young
Greek could aspire than that of teacher of his people
($\Delta\iota\delta\acute{\alpha}\sigma\varkappa\alpha\lambda o\varsigma$).　In the absence of any political career, it
promised the intellectual and moral supremacy always dear
to the Greek mind, and gave scope for the exercise of an
immense and most beneficial influence.　The lectures and
patriotic harangues of Gennadius became so celebrated
that they were attended by the Hospodar, the Boyars,
and their ladies, who at that time vied with each other
for distinction in Greek culture.　It was during one of
his most impassioned harangues that a messenger entered
the lecture hall, bringing to the Prince the news that
Ypsilanti had crossed the Pruth and raised the standard
of revolt.　Thereupon Gennadius, tossing his books and
papers into the fire, called upon his pupils to follow him
to the Greek camp.　The " sacred battalion " of Ypsilanti,
recruited from the noblest Greek families, was unhappily
almost all slaughtered at Dragachan ; but out of that
bloodshedding burst forth the revolution in Greece proper.
Thither Gennadius went with the survivors, and was
foremost in the ranks of the first regular Greek corps
formed by the French Philhellene, General Favier.　It
was at the battle of Karystos in Eubœa that he first
distinguished himself as a soldier, fighting at the side of
his commander and friend.　But it was chiefly by his

wisdom in council and his oratory in the camp that he won the admiration of his countrymen.

The Egyptian army which had invaded the Peloponnesus was menacing Nauplia. Within that fortress was crowded the remnant of the garrison of Missolonghi, with many helpless widows and orphans. Poverty brought discontent and internal discord, and the town was considered lost, when Gennadius stood up under the plane tree in the market-place and harangued the dispirited crowd with such power that the men felt again animated to self-sacrifice and heroism. Money being wanted to organise a cavalry corps, he placed his watch upon the stone by the tree, and emptied thereon what few coins he possessed, crying aloud, " Now do I bind myself publicly to serve gratis as a teacher in the family of any one who will here deposit some gold pieces." Thus he obtained control over those who only wanted a stout heart to guide them. He ordered all available horses to be seized ; money flowed in freely ; the demoralised soldiery were formed into an army, a cavalry regiment organised, and the Turks repulsed in a sortie which ended that year's campaign. For this and other signal services, Colocotronis and the rest of the chieftains wished to confer upon him at the end of the war the rank of a general. But, in that quiet self-effacing manner which contrasted so forcibly with his fiery zeal when the public good was to be served, he declined it, saying that he knew not how to lead men to battle, but only how to make them good citizens, and devoted his efforts to organise that admirable system of gratuitous public instruction which is one of the proudest achievements of modern Greece. Later on he declined the urgent invitations of King Otho to accept the post of Minister, objecting again that he was fitted not for politics, but instruction. His moral power was, however, supreme in Greece, and his authority and influence was felt wherever the Greek language was spoken, both in the East and the West. From every centre of national activity he was appealed to. Bishops and Cabinet Ministers

T

were proud to call themselves his pupils; and the word of "the Master" was all-sufficient. Through his instrumentality many of the public institutions which adorn Athens were raised and endowed by the munificence of rich Greeks living abroad. Large sums were constantly intrusted to him for these objects; and although, from his scanty means, the strictest frugality was necessitated to rear his numerous family, he yet continually helped on struggling students; and when his wife, a scion of the old and noble Athenian family Venizelos, withheld from his too-open hand even his pocket-money, he could not resist the appeals of the many young Greeks who gathered round him, but gave out written orders for books, clothing, &c., thus incurring debts which, amounting to a large sum, were paid after his death by his executors.

His influence was at its highest when, during the Crimean war in 1854, Epirus, his native land, rose in revolt. He was at once proclaimed President of the Revolutionary Committee, and threw himself into the sacred cause of liberation with all his old fire and enthusiasm. But the action of the Powers, ever opposed to the extension of Greece, broke his heart. The excessive toils to which he had exposed himself, regardless of his advanced age, conjoined to the pain he felt at the suppression of the revolt by the Powers, had exhausted his powerful frame, and in November 1854 he fell a victim to the cholera, which was supposed to have been brought to the Piræus by the foreign vessels who occupied that port.

The consternation at Athens was so great, and the number of interments so hastily made, that his funeral was necessarily a hurried one, and it was feared that the spot was not precisely marked. The indignation felt that no tomb had been at once raised was great, and it is to this painful incident that reference is made in the opening lines of the Elegy.

[The above sketch of his father's life is from the pen of Mr. J. Gennadius, the present Greek Minister, London.]

APPENDIX.

NOTES.

(*See* Note 3, page 40.)

Ξεφτέρι = *vulture* = *hawk* = *falcon*, and metaphorically = *soldier*. This word, more than any other perhaps, has been subjected by translators to the most varying definitions. A bird of prey is, however, the correct signification ; and an unclean bird like the vulture would seem to be specially indicated, if the word Ὀξύπτερος, alluded to in the Epistle of St. Barnabas (Hegele's edition of the Apostolic Fathers, Tübingen, 1839), be identical with Ξεφτέρι. The passage runs—"Οὐ φάγεσθε χοῖρον, οὐδὲ ὀξύπτερον, οὐδὲ κόρακα," Pars. i. Pect. x. Falcon, however, or hawk, is more applicable, as used by the poets as a synonym for warrior. A Greek lady well acquainted with the dialect of Ætolia and Acarnania derives it from the Latin "Accipiter." I quote her words : "Ὁ νῖσος (Κοινῶς Ξεφτέρι) εἶνε εἶδος ἱέρακος (γεράκι) Ἡ λέξις ξεφτέρι γίνεται ἐκ τῆς λατινικῆς Accipiter," and refers to Koracs, who, in his "Ἄτακτα" (1 τομ. σελ. 243, 2 τομ. σελ. 128), explaining the word Ξεφτέρι, says it is a *barbarous* word—"Ἐξεφτέριον—καὶ Ξεφτέριον, βάρβαρος λέξις σχηματισμένη ἀπὸ τὸ Ρωμαϊκόν." The word occurs in the poems of Πτοχοπροδρόμος in the twelfth century. It has been suggested by Miss M'Pherson that Ὀξύπτερος may have been confused with Accipiter, which would account for the position of the accent. Hawk, sparrow-hawk, and falcon are the only admissible renderings for the word. Alexander R. Rhangabê, in his *Histoire Littéraire de la Grèce Moderne*, vol. ii. p. 255, translating a passage from "Τὰ Κρητικὰ" of Aphentoulês, gives the following—"Mais mon intrepide aiglon n'a pas bongè d'un ponce de mes côtés" for the original "Μὰ πιθαμὴ δὲ σπάραξε τ' ἀθανάτο ξεφτέρι ἀπὸ τὸ πόδι μου κοντά." Professor Blackie, in an article entitled "Romaic Ballads" in the *National Magazine*, 1857, translates the first three lines of the ballad of "Tsamades" (No. cclvi. of Passow's *Carmina Pop. Græciæ R.*)—

> " Ν' ἀμοῦν πουλὶ να πεταγὰ, νὰ πάω στο Μεσολόγγι
> Νὰ διῶ, πῶς παίγουν τὸ σπαθὶ, πῶς ῥίχνουν τὸ τουφέκι
> Πῶς πολεμοῦν τῆς 'Ρούμελης τ' ἀνήκητα ξεφτέρια,"

Thus—

> " Were I a bird with wings, to Missolonghi would I fly,
>   To see how there with sword and shot they lay the Giaours low,
>   And sweep the bold Roumeliotes like *hawks* upon the foe."

Dr. Theodore Kind, in his *Handwörterbuch der Neugriechischen, S.* (Leipzig, 1876), besides giving Geier as the German for Ξεφτέριον, gives a verb Ξεφτερίγω = *sie federn aus reissen.*

The most strange interpretation of this word is to be found in Passow's vocabulary to his *Carmine* — " Ξεφτέρι (ἐξαπτέρυγος), *Angelus sex alis ornatis.*" Pouqueville also, who resided fifteen years in Epirus, in his ornithological list at the end of his *Histoire* has the following :—" Coucou, cucullus canorus, κόκκυξ, Π Δεκοκτο, κοκοῦ, Ξεφτέρι, τριγωνουράτος."

" PARTRIDGE "—a favourite simile.

(*See* Note 2, page 40.)

THE number of love-songs of the people in which the partridge is employed as a tender epithet, and partridge-eyed (περδικομμάτα) as a complimentary designation, is considerable. The two following examples may suffice to show how it is applied. The first is " The Klepht in Love " ('Ο 'Ερωτευμένος Κλεφτής), from the collection of Michaelopoulos, p. 191 :—

> " 'Απόψε δὲν 'κοιμήθηκα, καὶ σήμερα νυστάζω,
>   γιὰ δυὸ ματάκια γαλανά, γιὰ δυὸ γλυκὰ ματάκια."

> " This night I have not slept, and to-day I'm very drowsy,
>   Because of two blue eyes—of two eyes looking sweetly.
>   Some dark night I will steal them, when no moon's rays are
>   shining,
>   And bear them to the hill away, to the top peak of the mountain ;
>   And at midnight I will kiss them—will kiss them oft and quickly,
>   While the *partridge* sings its song, and the nightingale too
>   singeth.
>   Three times the lambs have bleated, five times have cried the
>   peafowl.
>   Awake ! my girl with *partridge eyes*—awake, and come thou
>   with me,
>   And I will kiss the little mole that on thy cheek thou wearest."

The next is "The Cool Spring" ('Η Κρυόβρυσι), Michaelopoulos, p. 351—

> " Σαράντα πέντε Κυριακαῖς, σαράντα τρεῖς Δευτέραις
> δὲν εἶδαν τὰ ματάκια μου τὴν κόρην π' ἀγαποῦνε."

" Five-and-forty Sundays, and three-and-forty Mondays
Mine eyes had never looked upon the girl whom I loved dearly,
And yesterday I saw her, who amid the dance was dancing ;
Her eyes were cast adown, but all over she was smiling,
And once, when 'mong the many more who passed in line before
    me,
She openèd her lips, and then to me she murmured softly,
'To the cool spring I will come to-night, and there we will
    betroth us.'
What can she to her mother say, and how can she deceive her ?
What pretext can she find to go alone unto the fountain ?
' Mother, no water have we now wherewith to drink this evening.'
' Daughter, there doth the pitcher stand—canst thou alone not
    venture ?'
She took the vase and ran along like as *a partridge* swiftly.
Her heart beat loudly on the way as to herself she reasoned—
' If at the spring alone I am, and find my love there sleeping,
What can I do that he may see me ? how can I him awaken ?
To kiss him I should be ashamed—I tremble to caress him—
With water to besprinkle him I fear, lest it might chill him.'
She found her lover wide awake, alone, beside the fountain.

She found her mother fast asleep, for late had grown the
    evening."

THE BELL.—(Τὸ Σήμανδρον.)

(*See* Note, page 94.)

"Græci etiam apud Turcas degentes, quippe qui Turcico Imperio subiecti sunt, campanis carere iubentur, campa umq. loco, tabula quadam lignea, malleis duobus ligneis prænotata, quam Symandrum, vel Synandrum ab hominum Cœtu conuocando dictum appellant, & Ferrea item lamina cum ferreo malleolo concinnata quam 'Αγιοσίδηρον —Hagiosiderum—hoc est, sanctum ferrum, vocant, vtuntur, dum nonnulli tanquam Campanarij ante fores Templi in edito loco Populum ad Templum conuocant, ut Hieronymus Magius dicto in libello scriptum reliquit. 'Campanorum autem vsum a Turcis vetitum esse Græcis, constat eo, quòd Campanarum sonus nimiam securitatem, et auctoritatem præfeferat, et valde ad coniuratorum, aut seditiosorum animos, quamuis longè, latèque—dispersos contra

Turcam de improuiso congregandos existat idoneus.'"—*De Campanis Commentarius*, F. Angelo Roccha, Episcopo Jagastensi, 1612, cap. I.

Stephen Durant, in his *Ritibus Ecclesiæ*, compares the destruction of bells by Huguenots and Saracens—"De Religione Turcarum vsum Campanarum nequaquam admittunt ; Illisq. etiam ipsis Christianis, qui sub ditione eorum viuunt, prohibent." He also shows how similar in this respect is the conduct of Turks, heretics, and demons—"Quæ pro-fecto, cum ita sint, Hæreticæ ac Turcæ magnam similitudinam & conuenientiam habent cum Dæmonibus qui sonitum campanarum tantopere abhorrent."

FESTIVAL DANCES AND DANCE-SONGS.

(Allusions to pages 75, 238, 249.)

THE great festival of Easter still affords the traveller an opportunity for seeing the picturesque dancing of the women in every village ; but Megara, from its accessible distance from Athens, draws the greatest number of visitors. The beauty of the women of Megara, of which I heard so much from Athenian gentlemen, appeared to me over-estimated. Their good looks consist in a fresh complexion and fine eyes, to which may be added the charm of a very modest demeanour, their eyes being mostly downcast throughout their dancing. The dance is but a slow rhythmical movement ; and as the line of girls advances and retires, holding together by a kerchief in their hands, the waving of a long line of some twenty, thirty, or more girls and women in their holiday costume of embroidered jackets, skirts, and aprons, and floating gauze veils surmounting their coin-decked brows,[1] has doubtless a charming and poetical effect in the scenery in which it takes place. The songs which accompany these dances, sung in a low voice, are very varied in character, and some very old. In the collections of Aravandinos and Passow they are to be found of every type. Many are as expressive of hatred to the Turk as the two lines, page 76, in "Our Grandmother's Girlhood." The most of them are, however, love-songs—some plaintive, but generally sprightly or saucy, in which the old Greek personification of natural objects (προσωποποιία) is prominent—lemons, oranges, birds, &c., being used as loving epithets or types. As many of these have been presented in "Folk-Songs," I will merely allude to one that, in its connection with the so-called *sun-myths*, has received some attention from writers on that subject. A maiden likens herself in her beauty to the sun in

---

[1] "γυαλιστάρα"— three or four rows of silver "παράδων," paras.

its power and glory ; the latter withering the green herbage when it appears in all its strength—the former, when she goes forth in her ornaments, annihilating the Pallikars ; for example, in "The Little Rose" (Τὸ Τριανταφυλάκι), the girl, having decked herself with twelve rows of sequins (φλωριά)—six rows twined around her neck, and six round her head—calls upon the sun to come out with her and shine—"shine as I will shine," adding, "πολλαῖς καρδιαῖς νὰ κάψω"—"I shall burn up many hearts"—

> " Καὶ σὺ ἄν λάμψης ἥλιέ μου
> Μαραίνε τὰ χορτάρια
> Κ' ἐγὼ ἄν λάμψω ἥλιέ μου
> Μαραίνω παλληκάρια."

The two following distichs, which Mr. Drosinês heard at the dancing in Eubœa, contain very favourite conceits, and are not in the usual collections, although they possess many with similar ideas :—

> " Η θάλασσα τρώει βουνὰ καὶ τὰ βουνὰ λειοντάρια
> Κ' ἡ μαυρομάταις καὶ ξανθαῖς τρώε τὰ παλληκάρια."

" The sea consumes the hills, and the hills the savage beasts,
And the black-eyed and the fair ones consume the Pallikars."

> " Σὰν κτενιστῆς Ξανθοῦλα μου δός μου τ'ἀποχτινέδια
> Γιὰ νὰ τὰ πάω̈s τὸν χρυσικὸ νὰ φτίαση δακτυλίδια."

" When thou combest thyself, Xanthoula, give me the combings, and I will take them to the goldsmith, that he may make me rings therewith."

THE PANAGIA.

(Page 141.)

ACHILLES PARASCHOS in this little poem has embodied in a certain tender simplicity the more familiar aspect of affection, as borne by the Greek peasant to the Blessed Virgin, rather than the reverential devotion taught in the Orthodox Church as to one "more honourable than the Cherubim, and beyond compare more glorious than the Seraphim." It contains all the character of the sacred folk-songs of this type. As an illustration of the manner in which the archaic custom of votive offerings still lingers in the Eastern, as in the Western (Latin) Church, I give the following from the Anthology of Michaelopoulos, entitled "Η Βοσκοποῦλα" (The Shepherdess) :—

" Μιὰ Βοσκοπούλα ῥοδοπλασμένη
        Τ' ἀρνί της χάνει στὴν ἐρημιά."

" A ruddy, rosy shepherd maiden
        Lost her lamb in pathways lone,
    And despairing, down the hillside
        Running, calls with piteous moan—

" '*Levke !*[1] Light of mine ! where art thou ?
        Speak'st not—hear'st not me deplore ?
    Ah, dear God ! I've lost my lambkin !
        Pitiest thou not, nor lov'st me more ?'

" Through the valley hastes the damsel
        With her loosened golden hair,
    And 'mid tears, her hands uplifting,
        Crieth to Panagia fair—

" ' Panagia ! sweetest virgin,
        Show me where doth Levke hide,
    Soon then—soon with wreathen flowers,
        Tapers white I'll bring beside.

" Panagia ! do this marvel,
        And a lamb I'll make for thee
    All of silver, which suspended
        Shall o'er thy sacred picture be.'

" When God brought again the dawning,
        Dancing, laughed the shepherd maid,
    For, held within her arms, was fondled
        Like a dove the lambkin strayed."

Notwithstanding the endeavours of folk-lorists to identify the archaic worship of Athene by the Pagan Greeks as one with the reverence paid to the Blessed Virgin (Παναγία) by the modern Greek peasant, I cannot but regard their deductions otherwise than forced and overstrained. The desire to prove too much is very evident. No Greek peasant, however ignorant, could confuse his orthodox teaching so far as to confound the respect or devotion the Orthodox Church impresses upon him as due to the Θεοτόκος with the idea of sacrifices as paid in olden times to Athene. To roast a lamb *to her* on *Good Friday* is almost too preposterous an idea to be alluded to, had not it been made an opportunity for a reviewer to animadvert upon the odd mixture of Pagan and Christian ideas jumbled together in a folk-song : by error in translation.[2]

---

[1] Λεύκη = fair one = white.   [2] *Bookseller*, June 1885.